THIS LAST MISSION

A Love Story Written by a Retired Air Force Pilot's Wife

A Novel

THEDA YAGER

WESTBOW PRESS®
A DIVISION OF THOMAS NELSON
& ZONDERVAN

Copyright © 2019 Theda Yager.

All rights reserved. No part of this book may be used or reproduced by any means, graphic, electronic, or mechanical, including photocopying, recording, taping or by any information storage retrieval system without the written permission of the author except in the case of brief quotations embodied in critical articles and reviews.

This is a work of fiction. All of the characters, names, incidents, organizations, and dialogue in this novel are either the products of the author's imagination or are used fictitiously.

WestBow Press books may be ordered through booksellers or by contacting:

WestBow Press
A Division of Thomas Nelson & Zondervan
1663 Liberty Drive
Bloomington, IN 47403
www.westbowpress.com
1 (866) 928-1240

Because of the dynamic nature of the Internet, any web addresses or links contained in this book may have changed since publication and may no longer be valid. The views expressed in this work are solely those of the author and do not necessarily reflect the views of the publisher, and the publisher hereby disclaims any responsibility for them.

Any people depicted in stock imagery provided by Getty Images are models, and such images are being used for illustrative purposes only.
Certain stock imagery © Getty Images.

Scripture taken from the King James Version of the Bible.

THE HOLY BIBLE, NEW INTERNATIONAL VERSION®, NIV® Copyright © 1973, 1978, 1984, 2011 by Biblica, Inc.® Used by permission. All rights reserved worldwide.

ISBN: 978-1-9736-5111-6 (sc)
ISBN: 978-1-9736-5112-3 (hc)
ISBN: 978-1-9736-5110-9 (e)

Library of Congress Control Number: 2019900512

Print information available on the last page.

WestBow Press rev. date: 2/19/2019

My tribute to Military

This Last Mission is dedicated to my military family and friends, past and present. I come from a very long line of military service members. Here is a list of some of them: my great-grandfather was in the Civil War, uncle in WWI, my father and two brothers, one brother-in-law, cousins and numerous uncles in WWII, two brothers in Korean War, my husband was in the Vietnam War and son-in-law and various nephews have been active duty until the not too distant past. All services have been represented in our family except for the Marines.

My father and three brothers and two brothers-in-law were Navy, one brother, Army, a son-in-law was in the Coast Guard and a nephew and niece were in the Air Force as was my sweet husband, Donald E. Yager, who was in the Air Force for twenty-six years.

Through the years we have made friends in all branches of service. As a C-130 pilot, my husband was assigned to numerous Air Force operational units in the United States and overseas. Also, he served at the Air Force Staff College in Alabama, CINCPAC Head Quarters in Hawaii and at the Armed Forces Staff College in Virginia. We were privileged to meet many service personnel outside the Air Force units to which he was assigned.

Most of the civilian community has no way of knowing how much effort military personnel and spouses put in as they attempt to keep marriage and homelife alive. Nor can they possibly understand how difficult it is to maintain relationships with their spouses and the children who miss the serving parent amidst numerous deployments. Military family life is an evolving, growing organism. The military person is building a career and has a growing family, while the spouse may have a career while trying to keep the family together along with dealing with various children issues. The challenge to maintain a balance between family and military duty is not an easy assignment for the member in the military.

A common story military spouses share is how long the military member has been deployed when the first crisis happens. One such time, our three small daughters and I had dropped Don off at the airport for him to fly back to South East Asia and the car broke down before we could drive home.

Military children miss the experience of an extended family. Grandparents may only be visited once a year. There is not the close-knit ties that their civilian cousins may enjoy with an extended family.

To this day we maintain contact with many military friends, both NCOs and families and families of commissioned officers. The key to it was wonderful, lasting love and friendships with Christian brothers and sisters connected with the military.

I wish I could include all the stories and struggles our family and military friends have endured for the love of God, family and Country. Since that would be impossible, I have created a fictious family who represents some of the people we have loved and respected through the years. While this book may not answer all the readers' questions about military families and military life, hopefully, the reader will have a better understanding of what is really involved, to some degree, as these characters try to make the best of each situation they encounter as they serve their country.

My sincere thanks to our-son-in-law Donald C. Wingard, (CWO4 USCG, Retired) who was stationed aboard the U.S. Coast Guard ice breaker, the Polar Star. He provided information about what *might* have happened aboard an ice breaker, even on the civilian ice breaker, in my fictitious story.

Again, thanks to my husband Donald E. Yager, (Colonel USAF, Retired) for making suggestions, reading and re-reading my latest manuscript. He is a good sport. He only reads my manuscripts after they are completed. He has not seen them until the last paragraph is written. It is always good to have a second set of eyes to read what has been written. It does get my attention when he says, "Is this what you *really* meant to say?" Yes, that does get my attention because it means back to the drawing board and perhaps a re-write of that portion of the manuscript and a re-read for him.

Chapter 1

Consuelo sat and watched her husband pack his flight bag and then dress. The mission was for an undetermined number of days to an unspecified location. Her air force husband could not tell her where he was going or how long he would be away. She was a seasoned military wife. She knew not to ask.

Jeff was a B-2 bomber pilot. He had a system for packing his flight bag—yes, even a checklist—to make sure no item was forgotten. She knew the routine, including which articles of clothing were packed first. Everything had a specific place and order in the packing process.

She watched as he placed a sports jacket, one pair of slacks, one dress shirt, four short-sleeved shirts, four pairs of walking shorts, flip-flops, dress shoes, a swimsuit, socks, a uniform, and other essentials inside his bag. He looked at her. Their eyes met, and he winked. She smiled and breathed a sigh of relief. She thought she knew which direction he wasn't going. But she wasn't sure if this alternative was a safe place for the love of her life.

Jeff was in his underwear. She watched his tan, muscular body as he kept packing. He had a rhythm and a flow to each action. Each of the missions had become more painful, and they dreaded the separation but knew this was what each had signed on to do. He had qualified and completed flight training and eventually earned his senior pilot's wings. And she had agreed to be an air force pilot's wife.

She sat quietly while trying to beat back tears as she became lost in memories of their lives together. She had to be strong. She didn't want to show signs of weakness and give him anything to worry about on the home front. Her professional job was a nurse practitioner for a cardiology team, and then, of course, her children, Peter and Deborah, would consume her time. She dreaded the lonely days and nights that lay ahead while she waited and wondered where he was and if he was safe.

She knew she would be notified if he wasn't.

He glanced at her. She was seated on the bed among the rumpled, warm bed covers with her feet tucked under her. She was staring off into space, deep in thought.

For a moment, he looked at her. She was still in her nightgown. He loved her long, dark hair cascading over her soft shoulders and her big, beautiful brown eyes. But now they looked as if tears could come out and spill down her lovely cheeks at any moment. He thought, Get a grip, Jeff. You have a mission waiting for you. Pull yourself together and get going.

She was thinking, Jeff is a ruggedly handsome, six-feet-two-inch-tall Navajo Indian from Chinle, Arizona. He is meticulous and accurate to a fault. She never worried about him making a wrong decision. That was not his nature. Everything he did was planned to the last detail—and then double-and triple-checked.

Consuelo, half-Mexican and half-German, was from Durango, Colorado. She had met her husband in college, where she'd been attracted to the tall, arrow-straight, handsome young man. He had applied to the US Air Force Academy but had not received an appointment; therefore, he began attending the University of Utah. He had completed his second year of college when he received an appointment to the academy.

Consuelo and Jeff had corresponded and attempted to keep the relationship alive over those years. But eventually the letters and contacts became less and less. Eventually, they stopped.

Consuelo graduated with a nursing degree and then earned an advanced degree as a nurse practitioner. She began working for a cardiologist in Durango. One day, the receptionist called her to the front desk, saying she had a visitor. When Consuelo walked into the waiting room, there stood Jeff in an air force uniform.

Jeff cleared his throat and then spoke to her. He asked a question the second time before she focused back to the here and now from her reminiscing.

He said, "Tower calling Consuelo. Do you copy?"

They looked at each other tenderly, and he said, "Will you please check on Margaret while we are gone? She is expecting their third child. Charlie Swaine is the mission commander on this trip. And another thing, if we receive an okay, I will call you when I can. It just depends on circumstances."

He was beginning to put on his flight suit. Each pocket had a zippered pocket with a specific purpose. Then he donned the flight boots.

He had told the children goodbye the night before, after the nighttime ritual of Bible reading and praying with the little ones. The small boy and girl always prayed, "God bless and protect our daddy."

During their prayers, Consuelo had glanced up at Jeff and saw his Adam's apple bobbing up and down as he attempted to swallow the frog in his throat.

Now he quickly walked down the hallway and into the children's bedrooms and kissed each little sleeping child. Soon he would be leaving the house—at 3:00 a.m.—for an early-morning flight. Each time Jeff left, Consuelo felt as if he were leaving a huge hole in her heart. Before departing he would hold her tightly in his arms and kiss her over and over and eventually tear himself away. Then he would pick up his hat and flight bag and dash out the door, not looking back.

The goodbyes were becoming more and more difficult.

Chapter 2

Consuelo dropped Deborah off at kindergarten and Peter at his elementary school. The first day their daddy was away on a mission, the children tended to be clingy. Then they gradually slid back into the usual routine.

At her place of employment, Consuelo focused her attention on the day's schedule. There was a heavy schedule ahead. Some of the more fragile patients were to be seen. She and the doctors knew the patients and many of their families. There was a certain small-town feel to the office, a personal touch that seemed to comfort and reassure many of the more seriously ill patients.

One patient, Mr. Wyrick, had been coming to see Dr. Gutierrez since the practice opened some twenty years ago. Through those years, his wife had died, and he had moved in with a son and daughter-in-law. Soon, Dr. Gutierrez knew the whole family.

Mr. Wyrick was on the schedule for ten o'clock. He always had a corny little joke to tell. He would laugh louder than anyone else at his own joke. The office staff loved him and would spend extra time with him and with whoever brought him to the office.

Consuelo scanned the list. Oh no! Mrs. Berkley was scheduled for eleven o'clock. Brace yourself, honey. Here she comes. Mrs. Berkley was a legend in the office. She was a large, overbearing woman who was very loud and angry. Nothing ever pleased her. She fussed at the nurses, doctors, and Consuelo. The office staff cringed when they heard her walk through the door.

This Last Mission

The first time Consuelo met her, Mrs. Berkley said, "Well! And who are you? I don't like people with dark skin and brown eyes. I don't trust them. Where is the girl who took care of me last time? Do you know what you are doing? Call the doctor. I don't want you in here. Don't you dare touch me, or I will sue the lot of you!"

The more she talked, the louder she became. Her face was bright red, and veins were standing out on her forehead and up her neck.

Standing some distance across the room from her and talking softly, Consuelo had attempted to calm her down, assuring her the doctor would be right in.

Mrs. Berkley shouted all the more. "Get her out of here! Get her out of here!" Then she collapsed onto the floor.

Consuelo opened the door and yelled for help, and then she worked on the woman. Two doctors rushed in. One said, "I see introductions do not need to be made. Mrs. Berkeley is not our easiest patient. Will someone please call for an ambulance? Consuelo, this has happened before. Please do not be upset. We will talk more later."

Mrs. Berkley was transported to a nearby hospital. She vented her anger on the ambulance crew and then the hospital staff. They were attempting to calm her down, saying she would have a stroke if she continued to carry on like that. They all knew her. They had dealt with her many times before. This time, once the medical staff had inserted an IV, the attending doctor gave her an injection of a tranquilizer. Soon she became rational. She told them that she had been off medication for anger episodes. The attending doctor admitted her to the hospital and called a psychiatric team to come and evaluate her.

Even though Consuelo's first experience with her had been a couple of months ago, it was still fresh in her mind as Mrs. Berkley burst through the door. Everyone braced for an angry outburst. Who would be her target this time? Wide-eyed, everyone looked at everyone else… just waiting.

Mrs. Berkley walked up to the receptionist and said, "I have a ten o'clock appointment. I believe it is with your NP Consuelo Blackhawk."

Consuelo was out of sight down the hallway. She turned to one of the nurses and said, "I'll give you fifty bucks to say you are Consuelo Blackhawk."

A doctor standing behind her burst into laughter and disappeared behind a closed door. The nurse quickly made a fast exit, leaving Consuelo all alone in the area. She was looking for a place to hide when the hall door burst open and in walked Mrs. Berkley—heading straight for her. Not sure what her next move should be, in her most professional voice, she said, "Good morning, Mrs. Berkley. You are looking well today. May I help you?"

Doors up and down the hallway opened a crack, so staff could see and hear what would happen next.

The answer surprised Consuelo. "Yes, dearie, I have an appointment with you. I believe if you check my folder, I am due to have an EKG today. Are you married? I see a wedding ring. Are you a military wife? I was a military wife. My husband was killed in Vietnam. Nothing ever hurt me as badly as that. I am afraid I have been angry at the world for taking my dear husband. I have seen the world as my enemy ever since I saw that official air force blue car pull into my driveway and when two men got out to deliver the worst message a military wife can ever hear. 'Your husband has been killed in action.' Something snapped in me that day, and I could not get back to being myself. There was a big black chasm between me and everyone I met. My main reason for this visit today is to come apologize to you. You were on the other side of that chasm the last time I was in here. I saw you as the enemy. Please forgive me. My psychiatrist said I will never get better if I do not apologize to everyone I have hurt with my angry outbursts. Please forgive me."

Consuelo had tears streaming down her face as she opened her arms. Mrs. Berkley rushed over for a hug. She said, "That is the first hug I have had in many years."

The door had quietly opened behind the two women and Doctor Zachery had heard and seen all. He was astounded at what he had seen and heard.

He said, "Mrs. Berkley, Consuelo's husband is a major in the air force. He is a pilot flying the B-2. We are delighted to see you feeling much better today. Let me take your blood pressure and see how you are doing today."

"No offense, Doctor," Mrs. Berkley said, "but can Consuelo take my blood pressure?" She looked at Consuelo and smiled.

"That is fine. I will check your file to see what you might need today."

"Sir, please forgive me for being rude to you all these years. I think I am just fine now. Consuelo gave me what I needed, a hug and kindness. I really do not need to have an EKG. That was done while I was in the hospital. I just used that as an excuse to get to apologize for my angry years. Thank you all for putting up with me all that time. I think I am back to being me. I am volunteering with various charities and trying to use the years I have left for good rather than fighting the whole world. I am not sure if this is appropriate or not, but Doctor, can I give you a hug? Consuelo, thank you. Goodbye for today."

Chapter 3

Consuelo picked up Peter and Deborah from school. Once back home, Consuelo made a cup of tea and began to prepare dinner for her little family. The children sat in the kitchen telling her all about their day. Then Peter said, "I miss Daddy. When is he coming home?"

Consuelo said, "Sweetie, I don't know when he will come home. I hope it is soon. Was there something you wanted to tell him? You can write him a letter and tell him what you have on your mind. Then, when he is home, you can give him your message."

Deborah asked, "Can I draw him a picture?"

"That is a really good idea."

Peter asked, "Mommy, can you write Daddy about your day?"

She didn't say anything but smiled and said, "That might be a very interesting letter. How about us making a mailbox to put letters in for Daddy? Then, when he comes home, we will have a surprise for him!"

The children were clapping their hands, dancing up and down saying, "Yeah!" Consuelo turned on the national news. The lead story was, "Breaking news: Three B-2 bombers have just landed in Guam…." The cameraman was using telephoto lens near the end of the runway and took pictures of the planes landing. She heard nothing else the reporter had to say. She thought, looks like I guessed correctly. As always, there is no secrecy where the news media is concerned.

She fed her children, bathed them, and led them through their bedtime stories and prayer time. The children were always careful to pray for their daddy. Then she fell into bed completely exhausted

This Last Mission

from a stress-filled day. She was floating into that twilight zone just before dropping into deep slumber when her phone rang. Quickly she answered it. It was Jeff!

He said, "I understand that the national TV stations have announced to the world that three B-2 bombers have landed on Guam. The boss said since they have done that to give you a call and say, 'Yes, that is where we are.' We are watching North Korea. Sometimes I worry about how the media spreads news and just how not so helpful that may be. How was your day?"

"Do you remember the difficult patient who has given our office so much grief in the past? She came in today."

"Who did she nail today? Please tell me it was not you again."

"Actually, it was me, only she came to apologize for giving us so much grief last time. She told us her story and why she hated the world and everyone in it. When you get back home, I will tell you about it. She has made a 180-degree turn and wants to use the rest of her years for the good of mankind, not for hate. Turned out to be a very special moment. You must be terribly exhausted after such a long flight. Are you at a hotel? Or are they having you stay on base?"

"We are staying on base. You know the drill when things are hot. How are the kids? Tomorrow night I will try to call before they go to bed. I want to talk with them too. I will call if nothing negative starts up. I hate to hang up. I really miss you. I hope we can get a signal to return home soon. Love you."

"Good night, Jeff. I love and miss you too. Sleep well. We are praying for you. While you take care of your job, we are doing our jobs too. Stay safe. Until tomorrow. Love you."

Chapter 4

Three weeks had gone by since Jeff's departure. One day at work, Consuelo received a phone call from Jeff. When she answered, he didn't answer. Instead, pornographic pictures of Jeff and a woman appeared on the screen. Her initial shock and horror soon turned to anger. She quickly turned off the phone. She was crying and did not know what to do next. She composed herself and went about her duties, constantly thinking about what she had witnessed. Then she thought, that man was not muscular, like Jeff. He looked a little like him, but that was not Jeff.

She turned the phone back on and really looked closely at the man. That definitely was not Jeff. Quickly she went to her boss and asked for a couple of days off because of family matters. She said, "I do not have anyone scheduled for the rest of the afternoon. May I leave early?"

She went to Walmart and bought a cheap phone and purchased two thousand minutes of phone service. Immediately, she went to Margaret Swaine's home. She wrote a note before exiting her car. Margaret met her at the door, crying her heart out. She had received a similar message. Consuelo handed her the note. "Turn off the location app, then turn off your phone. I believe we have been hacked. Come outside. We need to talk."

Margaret did as Consuelo had suggested. The two women discussed the horrific, raunchy, pornographic messages they had received. Consuelo said, "Margaret, if this is not enough to throw you into premature labor, I don't know what it would take. But just remember, those men are not our husbands.

"Can you go with me to the base? I want to talk with Colonel Harrison and explain what we have received. I turned off the location services on my cell. This may be useless and silly, but I even wrapped it in several layers of aluminum foil to block the phone from being traced. You might want to do the same thing. Then we will put them in an insulated container."

Margaret nodded her head, reentered her house, and did as Consuelo said. While Margaret was in the house, Consuelo called the squadron commander and requested a meeting. She stressed that it was urgent. Fortunately, he was in his office. His secretary transferred the call to his desk. Consuelo requested an appointment and said she thought Margaret's and her phones had been hacked. It was imperative, she said, that they discuss the matter with him in a secure setting.

He asked how soon she could be there. "As soon as I can drive to the base," she said. He said, "I will have an escort waiting for you at the main gate."

When Consuelo and Margaret entered Colonel Harrison's office, he said, "Let me see what you have." Consuelo said, "I am not a techie, and I wasn't sure how the enemy might track our phones. However, I am thinking someone has hacked Jeff's and Charlie's accounts. Therefore, Margaret and I disabled our location services, turned off our phones, wrapped them in aluminum foil, and placed them in this insulated container. That may be overkill, but we did it."

She removed the cell phones, and the two women began unwrapping them. Margaret turned her phone on first and handed it to the colonel. Consuelo did the same, only she opened the message from "Jeff."

"I know Jeff would never-never send me anything like this!" she said. "Also, Jeff has a muscular frame. This man is skinny. That man is not my husband."

The colonel took the two phones and called in several technology specialists. They began working with the phones, and they were soon successful in tracing the fraudulent text message. They found where the air crew's phones had been hacked and set up with bogus accounts. The enemy had located family members and had begun sending hurtful messages to create strife in the families. This would cause the pilots to be more concerned about family matters than their jobs of defending America.

Unknown to Consuelo and Margaret, the team called all three B-2 aircrews on secure lines. They were instructed what to do about their cell phones. They were told that Consuelo and Margaret were in the colonel's office and that Consuelo had discovered the bogus text message. This discovery would prevent further pain and emotional suffering. Also, it should prevent future technological interference from the enemy.

Jeff and Charlie Swaine were told their wives had purchased cheap phones from Walmart and had new numbers. These numbers were then provided to the two men. This would provide communication tools until a permanent solution was found.

Unknown to Consuelo and Margaret, the team called all three B-2 air crews on secure lines. They were instructed what to do about their cell phones. They were told that Consuelo and Margaret were in the colonel's office. Consuelo had discovered the bogus text message. This discovery will prevent further pain and emotional suffering. Also, it should help technology block future interference from the enemy.

The three aircrews were instructed to purchase cheap phones for the interim to use until technology specialists had resolved the issue.

Consuelo said, "Sir, I have heard my grandmother tell how pilots' wives were targeted by activist groups during the Vietnamese war. Activists contacted them by phone and told them their husbands were murderers, in addition to all sorts of vulgar stuff. They were harassed day and night. Nowadays, who would ever think that we could be targeted by a foreign government?"

"Consuelo and Margaret, thank you for bringing this information to our attention. We will be able to get this under control much quicker since you recognized the situation to be what it is—hacking by a foreign government. On behalf of the squadron, I want to thank you for calling me and alerting us to this cyber-attack. I will have an escort take you to the front gate.

Be safe, be alert, and thank you again."

Chapter 5

The two shaken women went back to their homes. They attempted to process what had happened and get on with their lives.

Consuelo went to school to pick up Peter and Deborah. The two children came bouncing out the door and leaped in the car. Both were talking as loud as they could. There was so much to tell their mother. They had had an exciting day.

Peter said, "Next month, we are to bring our daddies to school, so they can tell the class what their jobs are. Mama, do you think daddy will be back home by next month?"

Deborah said, "Mommy, Bobby brought tadpoles to school today. He had the best show-and-tell ever! Mommy, can I take tadpoles to school sometime? "After a brief pause, she continued, "Mommy, where do you get tadpoles?"

And so the conversation went as they drove home. On the way, Consuelo decided to stop into a Ben and Jerry's. Peter saw where they were and started clapping his hands. "I want a Chunky Monkey."

"Me too," screamed Deborah. "Oh, Mommy, thank you for our treat!"

The threesome entered the building. When ice cream was purchased, they sat by a window so that Consuelo could see their car in the parking lot. At this moment, just seeing the vehicle was a comforting sight for Consuelo. It was a symbol of strength and power, which reminded her of Jeff. The children were chattering away, and Consuelo was lost in thought.

Suddenly her new phone rang. She reached in her purse for the new phone. Peter said, "What is that? Why are you talking on that funny phone? Where is your phone?"

It was Jeff. "Consuelo are you alright?" he said. "We were told what happened and the way you took care of this serious incident. The colonel could not be more complimentary of you and your levelheaded treatment of the situation. It could have gone south for us as a couple if you had reacted as the average person might have. I love you, Consuelo. The colonel said that you told him, 'Jeff would never do something like this. I know Jeff didn't do this.' Thank you for those words of trust. It makes my job a lot easier when I know I have your trust and you have my back."

Deborah said loudly, "Is that my daddy? I want to talk with him. Dad-dy! Dad-dy! Dad-dy!"

Consuelo said, "Thank you, Jeff. I love you too. Deborah wants to talk with you. She has a lot to tell you."

"Daddy, Bobby brought tadpoles to school today. That was the best show-and-tell ever. Daddy, will you bring me some tadpoles?"

"That must have been very exciting. I would like to have seen all those tadpoles!"

Peter yelled, "I want to talk to Daddy too. Can I have the phone? Pleeassseeeee?"

Reluctantly, Deborah handed the phone to her brother. "Daddy, next month our class is inviting our parents to come to school and tell what their jobs are. Do you think you will be home by then? I would like it very much if you were. We are working on a surprise for you at home. I hope you will like it. I love you, Daddy. Here is Mommy."

"Hey, little buddy, love you too. I hope I am back home by then, but I do not know. I want to be there."

Consuelo took back the phone. "As you can see, many exciting things have happened today on the home front. Are you okay?"

"Yes, I'm fine. It is just a cat-and-mouse waiting game. We are hoping against hope and praying with all our might that we do not have to take-off unless it is to return home. We are playing a lot of bridge waiting for the other shoe to fall."

This Last Mission

"Oh, Jeff, we are praying that cool heads will prevail and that the enemy doesn't 't decide to escalate the rhetoric with his threats. I hope he doesn't sling any more missiles toward Japan and Guam. The world is holding its breath. Please take care of you. We look forward to the day when you can come home. Changing the subject, I will use this phone until security tells me my regular phone is safe to use once again. Right now, I am very cautious about ever using it again."

"Where are you and the children?"

"We stopped by Ben and Jerry's for ice cream. Both children wanted Chunky Monkeys, as you may have guessed. I felt we needed a little treat after a rather rough day."

"Did you go to work today?"

"Yes, I went to work. That is where I received the message. I asked for the rest of the day off as well as a couple more days this week. I needed to process what I saw on that phone. I had to get away from work and think through the problem and decide what to do. I couldn't use my phone to call anyone. I had to do that in person. I just had a gut feeling that the phone had been hacked. And if my phone has been hijacked, maybe your phone has been hacked as well. Anyway, after the trip to Walmart to pick up this phone, I decided to call Colonel Harrison, and then I went to see Margaret. She was crying hysterically when I knocked on the door. She had opened the 'message.' I wrote a note and had her read it. I told her to disable the location services, turn her phone off, and wrap it in aluminum foil. Silly idea, but I did it anyway. Then we put our phones in an insulated container and went to the base. You know the rest of the story."

"Well, I am proud of the way you handled a very raunchy and vile message. Colonel Harrison is very impressed. Because of what you did, you headed off a very serious hacking problem for all the aircrews. Honey, it was widespread. Not everyone has handled it as well as you. Some couples have experienced serious wounds over accusations and angry words that were said. Hopefully, they can sort out and heal the problems in their marriages. Security has traced the problem to North Korea. This is a far-reaching problem. The tech people will be working late into the night, and perhaps many nights, because of your quick decision to get to the bottom of this problem. The solution will arrive sooner because of it.

"I had better let you go. I am sure the ice cream is gone by now and you may soon need to go back to Walmart and add more minutes to your phone. The children may be getting restless by now. Wish I was there with you. I would like a Chunky Monkey too!"

"I wish you were here. The children are working on a surprise for you. We think about you in everything we do. Stay safe. Just know we are thinking about you and praying for cool heads to prevail where the North Korean situation is concerned. I hope we can talk again soon. Love you."

As they were saying their goodbyes, Consuelo could hear the alert horn sounding over the phone. Jeff quickly said, "Goodbye, honey. Love you. Gotta go." And the line went dead.

Consuelo sat in stone silence praying for his safety and for all the other pilots and military personnel who were scrambling to their duty stations and airplanes to face impending danger. She prayed silently that it was a false alarm and not a real and present danger to America—or one of her allies. In her mind, she saw him racing for his plane along with Charlie to do what they were well trained to do.

She gathered her things and took her children home. Dinner would be late tonight, but the ice cream would tide the children over. She wanted to turn on the TV but didn't want the children to see what might be upsetting news.

As soon as dinner was over, the usual bath and bedtime ritual was followed with special prayers for Daddy and his airplane. After hugging, kissing, and tucking in both children, she went to her room and turned on the television. The national news service was saying that North Korea had fired a rocket. It had gone high into the atmosphere and then plunged harmlessly into the Pacific Ocean. The danger was over—for the moment. She bowed her head, thanked God, and prayed that Jeff and the other flight crews would make it safely back to base. She thought, Jeff is such a thoughtful man. If he can, when he returns to the base, he will call and say all is well.

And he did.

Chapter 6

Consuelo had been thinking about the wives of the other deployed B-2 aircrews. She called them to see if they were okay after receiving the disturbing message. After visiting with them, she decided to host a luncheon in two days. She then called them back and firmed it up. They planned a menu for their little luncheon, and each lady offered to bring a dish. Consuelo explained that she had taken a couple of days off from work and would make chicken enchiladas. On the day of the luncheon, she would have a friend pick up Peter and Deborah. The wives were excited about getting together. She was happy about having the little get-to-gather. It had been a while since she had done something like this. Her work schedule interfered with daytime social events. She straightened up the house and began to make plans for the luncheon.

Finally, she collapsed in to bed and fell into a peaceful sleep.

When she returned home from taking the kids to school and back home, she had shopped. She began putting things away when the phone rang. Beverley, one of the wives she had spoken with the day before said she had a phone call from another wife, Sarah, who said, "Spouses in the entire squadron had received similar disturbing obscene messages. Some are not handling it well. They believe it to be real. Several couples were having serious marital problems before this happened and this has just about pushed them to over the emotional line."

Sarah asked Beverley if the other spouses who were not working could also attend the luncheon. "Oh my!" Consuela said. "I had better go back to the store! I had planned to make chicken enchiladas for the six of us! Who will call all these people? Will Sarah do that? Remind them it is set for eleven o'clock. I need to call Gerry Harrison and invite her. I think our little intimate sit-down-and-talk-it-out luncheon has exploded into a large group. Sure, let's do it! But I will need salads and desserts. Can you get that word out while I call Gerry? Oh yes, ask Sarah to get an approximate number of people who will attend. I need to know how many enchiladas to make."

This week of surprises had suddenly taken a new turn. Her mind was racing as she took inventory of what she had on hand and what she needed to purchase. But first, she had to call Gerry. She explained to Gerry that she had invited the wives of the other two aircrews who were with Jeff and Charlie to a little luncheon for the next day. Other wives had heard about it and wanted to be included. Suddenly, the small luncheon had turned into a squadron-wide luncheon. Spouses of other aircrews had received the same nauseating phone messages.

Everyone wanted to know how to handle the situation and to discuss the issue and just gain strength and support from one another.

Gerry said, "This is a lovely idea to get everyone together and discuss the problem. How are you handling food?"

Consuelo said, "I plan to have chicken enchiladas, salad, and desserts. Sarah is calling other spouses to see who might come and asking them to bring salads and desserts."

Gerry said, "Since this is a spur-of-the-moment luncheon, may I purchase paper plates, napkins, plastic glasses, and anything else we need? Let's make it a festive theme. Is that okay?

"Absolutely! I would appreciate you doing that!"

Gerry continued, "Some of these ladies need to have something light to think about. Their marriages were in trouble before these phone messages came in. Anyway, paper products, whatever the theme it turns out to be, will lighten your load. It may not be the way we usually do it, but this is a different situation. I will tell my husband. He may drop in too. You better make two or three extra enchiladas for him. Oh yes, is this set for eleven o'clock? Is anyone coming over early to help you get set up?"

"Yes, it is set for eleven o'clock, yes, and Beverly and Sarah are coming early to help."

"Good," Gerry said. "I'll call a couple other girls and get them to bring their card tables and chairs as well. So, don't worry about seating. You take care of the food. We will take care of the rest."

"Thanks Gerry. I appreciate your help. If your husband does come to the luncheon, will he please explain about the hacking of our husband's phones?"

Soon Sarah called saying it looked like 35 would be in attending. Consuelo thanked her, then dashed to the Commissary to purchase enough ingredients for approximately 50 large enchiladas. Thank goodness other ladies were bringing salads and desserts! The meal would be buffet style. She would be making pans of enchiladas until late tonight and stacking pans of them in the refrigerator.

She was very excited about everyone getting together. She thought, this is going to be fun. Yet, I'm just sorry it has to be under these circumstances.

Chapter 7

The night before, Consuelo had rolled the last enchilada at about 10:30. What a good feeling to have all that completed. Now, this morning, all she had to do was prepare beverages.

She dashed in and dressed for the day.

Gerry was there at 9:30. Margaret, Sarah and Beverley arrived right behind her and another car pulled in behind them. Doors flew open and women started carrying tables, chairs and food into the house. Everyone was chatting and giving quick hugs.

It is a good thing I have double ovens, Consuelo thought as she began to set out steaming pans of enchiladas and guests began filling their plates. There were only three or four ladies left in line when Colonel Harrison came popping in the door.

He said, "Consuelo, I heard you were making your famous chicken enchiladas. I couldn't let a little thing like being called a party crasher stop me from getting some of this luscious food! Hello, everyone. Glad you are here today. As soon as I eat my lunch, I want to visit with you about this nasty incident you have all been subjected to. Give me a couple ... five ... no, make it ten minutes or so to eat."

As soon as everyone had consumed their lunch, they sat waiting to hear what the colonel had to say. In the meantime, Consuelo said, "While the colonel is finishing his lunch, let me say how much I appreciate you coming to our home today. I am sorry this gathering is under such disturbing circumstances. We dependents are a team, just as our spouses are. We lean on each other for strength when bad things happen, and this qualifies as a crisis in my book! We are here to support and help each other recover from this horrific situation. I have invited Colonel Harrison to speak with us about this hacking incident. But first, thank you, Gerry, for your love, encouragement, support, and help preparing this impromptu luncheon. Colonel, the floor is yours."

"Consuelo, those enchiladas were just as delicious as I remembered! Thank you. I only ate three! As a result, its back to the treadmill for an extra thirty minutes for me! Folks, this has been some week. Thank you, Consuelo and Margaret, for coming to my office and drawing my attention to this matter. Prior to you contacting my office, we had not received information about this hack. Apparently, the messages were just coming in when Consuelo received her message. The enemy has hacked into our database and stolen flight crew information. They then mimicked military accounts, making you think those messages were from your loved ones. Their purpose is to distract our pilots by creating a rift with family members. Stirring up trouble with families is a means of emotional warfare. Do not fall for it! Do not take the bait. This is the enemy, not your loved one.

"We have contacted all ranks and levels of service personnel and alerted them to this problem. Thanks to Consuelo, we can directly discuss this issue with you at this luncheon. I repeat, do not swallow the bait. I repeat. These messages are from the enemy, not your loved one.

"Our security team is now building new programs to detect this type warfare. We are living in a day of technological warfare. You have been hit by one volley. Hopefully, it will not happen again, but we cannot guarantee it. Therefore, if you see anything unusual, let our security people know about it at once. The longer it goes unreported, the longer it takes to stop it.

"Thank you for letting me crash your party. I'd better get back to the office before my boss comes looking for me. I just hope no one told him about Consuelo's chicken enchiladas or he'll soon be here too." There was laughter throughout the room.

"Goodbye, everyone. I'll be in touch."

After he left, in small groups, the ladies began discussing what they had experienced. They discussed their anger and disappointment. Some had even called their spouses saying very harsh and hurtful things about what they had seen. Some had even used the big "D" word in their conversation.

Calmer voices now prevailed, as the women discussed how to begin making amends with their accused spouses. Some even discussed pastors or counselors who might help couples through the rough patches they had recently gone through.

Gerry sat with one group, Consuelo with another group, and Margaret with yet another. They talked until late in the afternoon and evening. The meeting eventually broke up. Hugs were exchanged, and tears were dried. Each person was assured that the team was there to support her. Much of the anger and hostility against the accused spouses had dissipated when they left for home.

After the last person had departed, Consuelo went to a neighbor's home to retrieve her children. She took the babysitter six of her famous chicken enchiladas as a thank-you for caring for her children.

Chapter 8

Saturday morning, Consuelo's phone rang. It was Jolene, a wife in the squadron. "May I come over?" she said. "I need to talk. I shared some at the luncheon, but my heart is so heavy, I need to talk with someone."

"Sure, come on over."

Consuelo told the children they could watch a children's show on the TV in her room. She instructed them to stay in the room because someone was coming over who was very sad and needed to talk grown-up talk.

Jolene arrived, and Consuelo could tell she was near the breaking point emotionally. She invited the distraught woman to join her in the breakfast area. She poured her a cup of coffee, and the two sat down to talk.

Words began pouring out. Her husband had been cheating on her for years. He spent the majority of his salary on other women, booze, porn, and strip joints. They attended counseling, but the problem didn't improve. Her husband only attended counseling sessions because he "had to," he told her.

"Other wives have numerous things their husband has brought from other countries. My husband brags about the women he meets in bars. He even showed me a list of their phone numbers at different bases he frequents. He has never brought our children gifts from when he was away. All our kids have heard is about the 'gorgeous women, not like their mother,' that he keeps company with. Consuelo, I have had to work to support our children. He spends the majority of his paycheck on his entertainment. I wanted you to know that last month I filed for divorce—yes, divorce—after more than twenty years. I am beat down. I cannot continue this charade any longer. We have not had a marriage in years. He moved out several weeks ago and is living in an apartment. The girls and I will be moving to a smaller house or apartment—something I can afford. I wanted you to hear the truth from me and not from the base gossip mill.

"Consuelo, I am devastated and cannot go on. I have even considered suicide just to escape from so many years of living with criticism, mental abuse, and disrespect. He would criticize me and humiliate me in front of people. I would gladly welcome death over what I have lived through these years. What can I do? Where can I turn? I came to you because I didn't know where else to go. At the luncheon, I felt safe in the group as we talked about the pornographic phone message. You didn't believe for a moment that Jeff would send you something like that. But I knew my husband would." Jolene sat weeping quietly, gasping out, "Please, help me. I do not want to go on living."

Quietly, Consuelo moved over and sat by the distraught woman. She held her in her arms. "Sit here. I will make a phone call or two. I will be right back. Would you like your coffee warmed up? Here is a pad of paper. Write down the names, ages, addresses, and phone numbers of your daughters, your family doctor, any other contact information you would like for me to have. I will need to call Gerry. After all, you are one of her girls. Do I have your permission to tell her what you have told me?"

Jolene, dabbing her eyes, nodded her head and began writing. After several minutes, Consuelo appeared and said, "Things are taken care of." She had made some calls, and Jolene would be seen by a doctor. She had arranged with the parent of Peter and Deborah's friends for a playdate.

After dropping off the children, Consuelo explained to Jolene that they were going to a doctor's office. He would be meeting them there, and she would be taken care of.

Consuelo looked at the woman in the seat to her right. She looked forlorn, like a beautiful flower now wilted—so hopeless, helpless, and vulnerable.

This Last Mission

When they pulled up to the building, Dr. Zachariah was on the sidewalk waiting for them. He gently escorted the two women into his office. Jolene filled out the usual paperwork for insurance, health history and names of contact persons. She wanted Consuelo in the room with her for the interview.

With the gentle skill of a caring psychiatrist, the doctor began the interview. When the process began, it was like opening a bottle whose contents were under extreme pressure. The years of hurt, anguish, disappointment, and feelings of failure spewed out. She described how nothing she did was ever good enough for her husband. He felt the same way about their children. No matter her successes or careful appearance, he found fault and compared her to some other woman who could do the same thing many times better. She told the doctor everything.

When asked if she had considered suicide, she replied, "Yes, many times. Death would be far better than the hell I am living in. At least I would be with my Lord and Savior, Jesus Christ, and have peace." Silent tears flowed down her pale cheeks and dripped onto her shirt.

He asked, "When was the last time you considered suicide?"

She whispered, "Just before I called Consuelo to see if I could come to her house this morning. And, I know you are going to ask me if I have a plan. Yes, I do. But instead of following through with it, I asked Consuelo to please help me."

Dr. Zachariah asked her to complete a little more paperwork while he made a couple of phone calls. Her motions were robotic as she filled out the rest of the paperwork.

Soon the doctor returned. "I have checked with my team. We are admitting you to a hospital. We will get you feeling better. You have a good friend to stand with you during this time, someone who knew what to do to get you help. Consuelo, if you two ladies will follow me in your car, we will go to Parkview Hospital. They have a room reserved just for you, Jolene. You will soon be on the road to recovery. Okay, ladies, let's go."

Chapter 9

Once back home, Consuelo called Gerry and told her that Jolene had been hospitalized for a possible mental breakdown. She would keep her updated on her condition. Gerry asked if Jolene's husband had been notified.

"I don't know where he is. He moved out weeks ago and lives in another house or apartment."

"Is he living with another woman or alone? Everyone knows how he is. Poor Jolene. She has put up with so much from him. Maybe my husband knows where he is. Legally he needs to know."

Consuelo quickly interjected, "Oh, she does not want him to know where she is! She feels in danger—if not from physical abuse from his verbal haranguing. He is not on the visitor contact list. The doctor will not allow him anywhere near her."

"When are visiting hours?"

"Not anytime soon. She is in the evaluation stage; I am not sure how long that will take. I will be checking in with the doctor. When I know, I will let you know."

Next, she called Molly and told her that her mother had been hospitalized for an emotional crisis.

Molly asked, "Have you called our dad?"

"No. I do not know where he lives, and, your mother has requested that he not be notified. She is fearful of his actions if he should learn where she is staying. I will call Janice and tell her what I have told you."

Molly said, "I can understand why Mother doesn't want him there while she is trying to get better. He would undo everything that has been done to help her."

Chapter 10

Sunday morning at church found Consuelo, Peter, and Deborah in their usual seats. Consuelo said she needed to hear God's encouraging words to help with the daily challenges. She felt recharged as she received hugs and encouraging word from fellow worshipers. Several asked about Jeff and said they were praying for all the aircrews and families during these turbulent times.

One wife said, "Anytime we turn on the news and hear about the threats and angry words being hurled back and forth, we stop and pray for peace and safety for our military brothers and sisters, as well as their families."

The weight of the load seemed to lift from her heart and shoulders as the congregation joined together singing wonderful songs of praise and thanksgiving.

The title of the pastor's sermon was, "Surely God is my salvation. I will trust in Him and not be afraid. The Lord, the Lord, is my strength and my song. He has become my salvation."

The pastor talked about, "In today's world we live in constant fear. Crimes of unimaginable proportions are happening daily, fear from national enemies, fear of being killed by bombs, knives, shootings, and drunk drivers on our highways. The sermon dealt with combating fear. In the Bible, 365 passages mention fear, yet it is always emphasized that He is our salvation."

The pastor said, "Put your faith in the Lord Jesus Christ. He is our guard, guide, shield and protector. God is always a whispered prayer away. He is never too busy to listen to your heartaches, fears, and pain. He will lead you through those difficult times. Hold on to his unchanging hand...."

Consuelo's mind drifted. *I needed to hear this message. This week has been so difficult. Lord Jesus, thank you for hearing my cries for help this week. It has been such a hard week. Please be with Jeff and the other military people who are protecting us. And please touch and heal the sick and suffering, like Jolene. Lord, thank you, Lord Jesus, for listening to me. Amen.*

She began listening once more just as the pastor said, "Repeat with me the twenty-third Psalm."

The Lord is my shepherd, I shall not be in want, He makes me lie down in green pastures,
He leads me beside quiet waters, He restores my soul.
He guides me in paths of righteousness For His name's sake.
Even though I walk
Through the valley of the shadow of death, I will fear no evil,
For You are with me; Your rod and your staff, they comfort me.
You prepare a table before me in the presence of my enemies. You anoint my head with oil; My cup overflows.
Surely goodness and love will follow me All the days of my life,
And I will dwell in the house of the Lord Forever.

The sermon continued with words of encouragement in combating fear and ended with the congregation standing and repeating the Lord's Prayer.

Our Father which art in heaven,
Hallowed be thy name,
Thy kingdom come,
Thy will be done on earth, as it is in heaven.
Give us this day our daily bread,
And forgive us our debts as we forgive our debtors.
And lead us not into temptation but deliver us from evil:
For thine is the kingdom, and the power, and the glory, forever.
Amen.

Chapter 11

Consuelo awoke with a start! Her alarm didn't awake them on time. She jumped out of bed and dashed down the hall, telling the kids to get out of bed and hurry. "My alarm didn't go off! We are late!"

She quickly made sandwiches and threw them into sacks along with chips and a cookie. She gave each child a breakfast bar to eat on the way to school. They managed to enter the door just as the last bell was sounding.

The freeway was a mess. She called the receptionist and told her that she was on the way and explained what had happened, promising she would be there as soon as she was free of traffic. When she dashed through the door, she felt disheveled. She whispered a prayer. Lord, things haven't started well. Help me this day with whatever is before me.

At ten thirty, her phone rang. It was Peter.

"Mommy, I was supposed to bring treats for everyone today, and you forgot!" She dashed into the office and said, "Is anyone available to run an emergency mission for me? My alarm didn't go off, and I forgot to take treats for Peter's class. I have everything sitting on the counter at home."

Julie spoke up and said, "I was getting ready to take a break. I'll do it. Give me your house keys." Consuelo: "I will call the school office to tell Peter the treats are on the way. Thank you, Julie. You are the best. I owe you big time!"

When the last patient was seen, Consuelo left to get the children from school. She felt as if she had been run over by a steam engine. As she was driving home, a phone message came from the hospital. It was one of Jolene's doctors. He was requesting a phone conference and wanted to know if this was a good time. She replied over the hands-free device, "Actually, I am going to pick up my children from school. Can I call you in thirty minutes? I will have privacy then, so my small children will not hear the conversation."

He agreed.

Once home and the children were settled in with activities, she resumed the conversation with the doctor.

He said, "Jolene had been severely depressed for a lengthy period. It will be a while before we have her stabilized. She is still on suicide watch. She was a very unhappy lady. I wish we could have gotten to her earlier but thank you for bringing her to us when you did. She is still not allowed phone calls or personal visits. I will notify you when you or her daughters can contact her."

Consuelo notified Janice and Molly and let them know that their mother could not receive visitors or phone calls. "The doctor will let us know when she is stable, and we can see her," she said.

Next, she called Gerry and gave her the same message.

Just as she completed the last phone call, Jeff called. She brought him up to date on all the happenings since their last contact. During the conversation he said, "I might be home in three weeks...maybe. At least we can hope so. Don't tell the children yet, just in case things go south over here."

After they had a lengthy phone call, Jeff said, "Can I speak to the children?"

Consuelo called out, "Peter and Deborah, your daddy is on the phone. Who wants to talk with him?"

There was a stampede of little feet down the hallway. Peter was the first one to the phone. He said, "Daddy, guess what? The alarm didn't go off this morning, and we were late. Mommy forgot the treats for school, and Miss Julie from Mommy's office brought the treats to us. Daddy, don't forget, in five weeks we are to bring our daddies to school and tell what they do at work. I want the kids to hear about your big airplane. Don't forget! Oh yes, bring pictures of your airplane. Oh, stop it, Deborah! Deborah is about to pull my sleeve off."

His sister snatched away the phone. "Hi, Daddy. Peter already told you all the good stuff about us being late. We ate a breakfast bar in the car. Joey brought a white rat to school. I was going to hold it, and it jumped out of my hand and ran under the teacher's chair. Then it ran in where we hang our coats and backpacks. Susie's backpack was on the floor. It ran in there and hid. That was so fun! Can I get a white rat? Please, Daddy, will you bring me a white rat? Here is Mommy. I love you."

Jeff was laughing when Consuelo took the phone. "That made my day! She wants me to bring her a white rat. Do you think she will settle for a toy one? Last time we talked, she wanted tadpoles. I hope no one brings a horse to school."

He and Consuelo enjoyed a good, hearty laugh over Deborah's antics.

Chapter 12

Two weeks had gone by since their last conversation. Consuelo was preparing the evening meal and had potatoes in the microwave. As she dashed about preparing the meal, there was a flash of light and a spewing sound. She looked around in time to see the area back of the microwave burst into flame. She screamed for the children to get outside. She grabbed her phone as she pushed the children out the door and called 911.

The fire department was there within fifteen minutes and were able to contain the fire damage to the kitchen, dining room, and breakfast nook. There was extensive smoke and water damage to the interior of the home.

Consuelo called Gerry and told her about the latest incident. She and Colonel Harrison soon arrived to give her moral support. Gerry called Margaret, who also came over with her two children. Neighbors had gathered in the yard. Peter and Deborah stood clinging to their mother and crying.

Many hours later, the fire chief came to Consuelo and said that he would accompany her into the house to retrieve clothes, personal items and children's school things. Then they asked her to leave. He suggested that she go to a motel or stay with a friend for the time.

Gerry and Colonel Harrison kept Peter and Deborah, while Consuelo went into the house with a fireman. The smell of smoke was heavy. She grabbed files of business records she would need to call the insurance company. Quickly she packed the children's suitcases, grabbed their backpacks, packed her own suitcase, and left the house.

Margaret said, "Come spend the night with us. We can figure out what to do next."

"Have you eaten dinner?" Colonel Harrison asked.

Lips quivering, near tears, Consuelo shook her head. "No, I was preparing the evening meal when there was an electrical fire behind the microwave."

"Okay, that settles it. Come on. We are going to get something to eat and discuss what to do next. Margaret, will you join us?"

"No, thank you. We have already eaten. I will go home and prepare for my three houseguests. See you later, Consuelo."

Over dinner, Colonel Harrison said, "Call the insurance company immediately. I will call Jeff and tell him you will talk with him later and that you are all okay. You might want to call your boss and let him know what has happened. There are many details to look after."

Gerry took Peter and Deborah to another table. She asked the server for paper and crayons. When the server brought them, Deborah looked up at him and said, "Our house just caught fire and burned."

The server said, "I am very sorry to hear that. Are you all okay?" He was assured they were all fine.

After Deborah's discussion with the server, Gerry entertained the children while her husband and Consuelo took care of business stuff. She ordered each child an ice cream.

Consuelo looked over and smiled. She thought, *How thoughtful and sweet!*

Mr. Whitmer, the insurance agent, said he would be at her house at nine o'clock the next morning.

Her boss said, "Take as much time as you need. We will reschedule your patients. If anyone cannot be rescheduled, we will work them in. Take care of this emergency. We will take care of things here."

She turned back to Colonel Harrison, who had a worried look on his face.

"Consuelo, I did not call Jeff. My office just called. Jeff and the other B-2 teams were on a mission. When you turn on the TV, you will hear about the latest provocation by North Korea. They launched another missile. Fortunately, it did not hit America or any of its allies. I'm happy to say it exploded not long after being launched. Our guys were already in the air when it happened. I'm sorry that you had to hear this latest stress our guys are under, especially after what you have been through tonight. You are made of good stuff, and so are our pilots. Jeff will be calling you once he is on the ground. Guess you will have to tell him about your day."

"Thank you, sir, and thank you, Gerry, for being here to support me this evening. We will get through this. I don't know how I would manage if it weren't for my air force family. At least no one was hurt. The house can be restored. It will just be a great, big, nasty inconvenience. We will be fine. I suppose I better get over to Margaret's house and get these children bathed and to bed. Thank you again for your support. I will update Gerry after I talk with the insurance adjustor at nine in the morning."

Chapter 13

Mr. Whitmer surveyed the heavily damaged kitchen. The kitchen and breakfast nook were gutted and charred, as were the entire wall and ceiling. The exterior wall and dining room were nothing but pieces of burned-through black charcoal studs where flames had entered the attic, damaged the rafters and flames had broken through the roof. Windows had blown out.

Other walls were damaged and blackened to a smoky color. The bedrooms had received heavy smoke damage.

Consuelo stood with the adjustor in stark amazement. "I had no idea a fire could spread so quickly and do so much damage. What will I do?" She began to weep. Awkwardly, he put his arm over her shoulders and patted her in an effort to comfort her.

He stepped away from her and said, "Electrical fires are like blow torches. The fire is extremely hot. Fire spreads quickly on dry wood. My company will house you and the children temporarily. It may be in Extended Stay America, since they have kitchenettes. Perhaps the military base has temporary quarters you can stay in while your home is being restored."

Consuelo said, "My husband is away on a mission. I do not know when he will return. He may be back during the time we are in the housing you furnish for us. If so, we need housing for four people. Will that be a problem?"

"No, not at all. Consuelo, I watch the news too. I understand. I am sorry you have this extra burden to carry. Military families are to be admired. I am not sure my wife would put up with all you military spouses, of all ranks, have to deal with, not to mention what our pilots and ground crews must endure. We will do our best to help you. I have a list of reputable companies you may want to contact to restore your home. There is extensive damage to an exterior wall and a structural wall, and in the attic and roof over the kitchen and dining room. This is not a quick fix. You will not be back in your home anytime soon. I might add that the smoke damage was so heavy, you will need new living room furniture and new bedding. The wooden pieces might be cleaned by a professional team. Floor coverings will need to be replaced. The only positive I can come up with is that when your home is restored, it will be like a new house. You can try to salvage any dishes, pots, and pans that might have survived the kitchen fire. Check the bathrooms and linen closet and see if the towels, sheets, and blankets can be cleaned and the smell of smoke removed. Take all the clothing to the cleaners and see if they can remove the smoke. You have a huge challenge ahead of you. Do you have a job? If so, you may want to take a leave of absence until you can get some of the more pressing matters taken care of."

"If a cleaning company can clean the wooden pieces, will I need to store the furniture while the house is being restored?"

He nodded. "Absolutely. I have the name of a good company who can help with that. Plus, they have people who will move and store the furniture for you. They are very accommodating. You can rent a portable storage unit, and have it delivered to your house and placed in the driveway to store things as you get them packed."

While they were talking, several neighbors, as well as Pastor Johnson, a homebuilder and a contractor from Consuelo's church, joined them.

Pastor Johnson said, "I had a phone call from Jeff. He is worried sick that he cannot be here and help in this crisis. He asked that I contact Michael Jameson and Carl Hatley. Jeff asked that I pull together a support team to help you get through this event."

Pastor Johnson introduced himself and said, "This is Michael Jameson from Jameson Home Builders, and Carl Hatley is a contractor. Jeff said you would be here, so we came to meet you since you are their insurance adjustor. I'm sorry we missed the evaluation of the damage to the home. Could we get you to do a recap? And may we go inside the house and see the damage?"

One neighbor said, "Let us take the sheets, bedding, towels, and other linens. We'll see, let us see if we can laundry them before you take all that stuff to a cleaner and pay a fortune. We can try. If it doesn't work, then send it out to be cleaned. I've heard of products that work very well on smoke odors. We can try."

Consuelo thanked them profusely as she wiped away tears.

To the neighbors, Consuelo said, "The smoke is so heavy in the house, I hate for you to breathe it. I will bring things to the door if you wait for a moment while I grab a load of towels and sheets. Then, Mr. Whitmer, I will join you and Pastor Johnson, Mr. Jameson, and Mr. Hatley. Go ahead and get started. I'll be right there."

Gerry walked up to the front door and said, "Hello, everybody. Looks like Consuelo has a lot of help."

One of the neighbors said, "Consuelo has gone inside to grab a bunch of towels, sheets, and bedding. We are going to try washing everything to see if we can get the smoke smell out. If we are not successful, then she can send everything to the cleaners. Pastor Johnson, Michael Jameson, and Carl Hatley are inside with the insurance adjustor. Pastor Johnson said, 'Jeff called and asked if he and Mr. Jameson and contractor, Carl Hatley, would come to represent him, saying Consuelo needs help.'"

"Hi, I am Gerry Harrison, the wife of Jeff's commander. We are all worried about Consuelo. She is a strong woman, but even strong women need a helping hand. Thank you for being such good neighbors. I heard you saying something about taking things to the cleaner. I called a dry cleaner. They said to just wash things in water to remove the smoke smell. Dry cleaning only makes the smoke smell worse. The dry-cleaning chemicals do not remove the smoky smell."

"That is good information to know. Very helpful. Oh, I'm sorry. I am Jane from next door. This is Betty from across the street. And who did you say you are?"

Consuelo came out the door with a mountain of towels and linens. Jane and Betty both broke into laughter. "I see two legs and a big stack of smoky-smelling linens," Jane said.

Consuelo laughed too. She said, "You two! Stop laughing and help me!" Both women started taking the load out of her arms. Consuelo was surprised when she saw Gerry.

"Hi, Gerry, Betty, and Jane, have you met Gerry Harrison? Her husband is Jeff's commanding officer."

Betty said, "We were just making our introductions when two legs with a truckload of linens came out the door." They all laughed again.

Gerry asked, "Do you have more things to bring out? Let me help you? I can take a load to my house too."

The task of the cleanup had begun.

Consuelo joined the men in the house as they surveyed the damage. The builder and contractor asked numerous questions as they did their examination, discussing the depth and severity of the damage.

The contractor brought in a ladder and investigated the attic to see how extensive the damage was there. The support beams across the apex of the roof were heavily damaged.

The insurance adjustor explained what his company would cover and what they wouldn't. The contractor asked difficult questions. The insurance adjustor rethought some of his estimates as the builder and contractor pointed out damage that he had not listed to be replaced. The discussion went on and on.

Consuelo stood listening and thought, Lord Jesus, thank you for urging Jeff to call our pastor. Thank you for sending Michael and Carl and for giving them the time to be here. Thank you, Lord Jesus, for your grace and kindness and wisdom.

Mr. Whitmer explained that he would have to return to his office and write the report. He would be back in touch with Consuelo as to when the estimate for restoration of her home could begin. In the meantime, Consuelo and her family would be temporarily housed.

Chapter 14

Once she was settled in an Extended Stay America apartment, Consuelo attempted to calm and comfort her children, trying to assure them that they would soon be in their home once again.

As they were beginning the bedtime ritual, Jeff called. He'd had a chance to speak with his son and daughter and to hear their bedtime prayers. Once the little ones were tucked in, he and Consuelo could have a long chat.

He said, "Don't say anything to the children, but I hope to be home before Peter's 'Bring Your Parent to School Day.' I have made a video. I used some Air Force promotional materials—with permission, of course—and I'm going to follow this with a video of myself addressing Peter and the class. But I hope to be home. This video is just a backup in case something goes awry. If things work out, I will be hitching a ride on a C-130 transport plane. I will keep you updated on that. Look for the little package in the mail. I mailed it yesterday. No, it is not a white rat or a tadpole—and certainly not a horse for Deborah! It is my video. Oh yes, one more thing. Did the insurance guy say how soon it will be before he gets back with an estimate?"

"The estimate will be in a few days. I do not have a specific date."

And, the conversation continued….

Margaret called about two o'clock in the morning, saying, "Consuelo, can you come stay with Johnny and Sarah? My water just broke. I am going to the hospital."

"Sure, I will be there as quick as I can. Who is taking you to the hospital?"

"I am driving myself."

"Oh, Margaret, I'll be there in ten minutes."

Consuelo called Gerry. "Sorry to wake you but Margaret's water just broke. I'm going to stay with her children, and she is driving herself to the hospital."

Wide awake now, Gerry said, "No, she isn't! I am on my way. I will take her to the hospital. I'll meet you there." Consuelo put on some jeans and a sweater, wrapped her children in blankets and stowed them in the car, and made a dash for Margaret's house. She and the children got there quickly, and they all rushed through the door. She placed Peter and Deborah on the sofa and set about helping Margaret. She said, "Gerry will be here in a minute. She is taking you to the hospital. I wish I could go with you."

Margaret had her bag in hand and started walking toward the front door. She stopped and clutched her belly in pain. She gasped. "Consuelo, I can't make it to the hospital. The baby is coming too fast!"

Consuelo guided her to her bed and had her get as comfortable as possible. "I am calling an ambulance," she said.

Gerry came dashing through the front door. "Where is she? Let's get going."

"She is going nowhere. She is getting ready to have this baby. Grab me some towels and hurry! The baby is coming!"

Gerry piled a stack of towels on the bed and Consuelo's training took over. A healthy baby boy soon made his appearance. By the time the ambulance arrived, the little guy was wrapped up and in his mama's arms, squawking that newborn baby cry, which is always music to everyone's ears.

Gerry said, "He has good lungs!"

Margaret, smiling and crying at the same time, said, "Thank you, Consuelo and Gerry. Meet little Tommy."

This Last Mission

The ambulance crew loaded mother and newborn in the ambulance and left for the hospital.

Gerry said, "Consuelo, I got here too late to be of any help."

"No, you did help. Had you not been here, who would have brought me this mountain of towels? Thanks for being here. Now to get all this bedding and towels in the washer."

"I'll call my husband and have him call Charlie with all the news. Goodness. This has been an exciting hour—well, a little over an hour. Do you know where the coffee pot is? I sure could use a cup. I am too wired to go home and go to bed."

A few hours later, Consuelo called her office and told them what all had happened since midnight. She explained that she was keeping Margaret's children until she could trade off with another wife. "Can I come in around noon?" she asked, explaining that military wives gather around one another when there is a need. Margaret's meals would be cooked, her children would be cared for, and someone would pick her and the baby up at the hospital as soon as they were checked over and released. Everyone would be helping her until Charlie returned home.

Days went by before Consuelo heard from Mr. Whitmer. He told her a check was being cut for the restoration of her house. Now the restoration could begin.

The next steps would be in Michael Jameson and Carl Hatley's hands. They had a contract saying how much the rebuilding would cost. Consuelo was overwhelmed with the decisions she had to make.

Gradually the process was begun. The furniture cleaning and restoration group arrived. Most of the wooden pieces could be easily cleaned. However, some pieces could not be restored; the extreme heat had scorched and falling embers had burned the wooden pieces. The dining room table and chairs had been destroyed, as well as the sideboard. Consuelo was thankful that Jeff had the wisdom to purchase replacement insurance for anything that was lost in the event of a disaster.

It was a painful process for Consuelo to see so many of her possessions scooped up and placed in a dumpster. Very few dishes survived. Slowly but slowly, she handled the decisions, remaining stoic as she watched item after item removed and placed in dumpsters.

Carpenters were removing charred and burned beams and walls. Doors and broken windows were removed. Soon a huge hole was visible across the back of the house. Once the destroyed area was removed, skilled carpenters would begin rebuilding the once beautiful home.

Betty, Jane, and Gerry returned the freshly laundered linens and clothing. Everything was boxed and placed in the portable storage unit. They had successfully removed the smoke smells. The restored furniture was cleaned and placed in the storage unit. Consuelo considered each little step as a leap of success.

Chapter 15

Peter was crying one evening. Consuelo said, "What's wrong, little buddy?" "We are living here, and Daddy cannot find us. The kids at school said, 'Your daddy can't find you. He doesn't know where you are. You are lost.' Mama, Daddy does not know where we are! I feel like we really are lost, and he can't find us. I want Daddy!" He sobbed uncontrollably.

By now, Deborah was crying tears of sympathy. Her brother was upset, so it had to be very serious, so she wailed too. "We are lost. I want my Daddy."

Near tears, Consuelo scooped both of her little ones into her arms and attempted to comfort them. She said, "Daddy knows where we are. He has our address. He knows that Mr. Whitmer and Mr. Hatley have begun to work on our house. I tell him everything."

"I want Daddy to be at my 'Take Your Parent to School Day.' I want my daddy," Peter said, continuing to sob.

Consuelo thought, I never call Jeff. I wait for him to call us. I think I will call and see if I can talk with him for a minute.

She picked up the little Walmart phone and dialed his number. He answered on the second ring. She said, "Did I call at a bad time? Did I wake you?"

"No, you didn't wake me, and this is a good time. What is happening?"

"I have a little boy who wants his daddy to know where we are. He feels like we are lost, and you cannot find us. Will you talk with him?"

Between sobs, Peter said, "Daddy, do you know where to find us? We don't have our home any more. It burned."

"Yes, little buddy. I know where you, Mommy, and Deborah are. I hope to see you before many more days. I don't know just when that will be for sure, but I hope soon. And I do know where you are. When I get home, we will go to Ben and Jerry's and get Chunky Monkeys. Is that okay?"

Deborah was pulling on Peter's sleeve. "I want to talk with Daddy too."

"Daddy, I have to go. Deborah is bothering me. She wants to talk with you too. Here Deborah, take the phone."

"Hi, Daddy. Peter was sad. He made me cry too. I want you to come home soon. Can you find us? Daddy, are we really lost, like Peter says?"

"No, little princess, you are not lost. I know where you, Peter, and Mommy are. I can find you. I hope to see you as soon as I can. Like I told Peter, 'As soon as I get home, we will celebrate by going to Ben and Jerry's and get Chunky Monkey ice cream.' Do you like that idea? Let me talk with Mommy, please?"

Deborah handed the phone to Consuelo. Jeff could hear Peter say, "Come on, Deborah. Let's go play. Daddy knows where we are. We are not lost."

"It looks like I may be heading home the end of next week, so long as nothing else breaks loose over here. Another aircrew is coming over to replace us. I can't wait to get home!"

"I hope I will have a good progress report on our house by the time you get home. I have taken pictures of each stage. I'll show you when you get here. It will be so good to have you home! I can't wait to see you. It seems like forever since you left."

The conversation continued for several minutes before the painful goodbyes.

She hurried into the bathroom as she turned off the phone, tears gushed out in a big cloud burst. She had held it all together until now; there had been a few tears because there had been so much pressure and stress bottled up. This time the dam had broken in a mighty release of emotions. She cried until there were no more tears.

Chapter 16

The big countdown was on: four days before Jeff was to be at Peter's school. This was the day he was to leave for the States. However, the plane he was to fly out on broke down at another base, so he would have to wait for another plane. Jeff was apprehensive, wondering if he would get home as planned.

The next day, the plane arrived and departed for Hickam Air Force Base, Honolulu, Hawaii. The crew day would end when they arrived. That meant they would spend the night and take off the next day for Travis Air Force Base, California.

Jeff's stomach was tied up in knots as he watched the clock. He was hoping and praying that no further problems would prevent him arriving in time to make his little son very happy.

The flight was scheduled to leave at 4:00 a.m. Jeff, along with several other GIs, boarded the plane. Hopefully, the next destination would be his home base.

The plane droned on. Nothing fancy about riding in the back of a C-130, but if it would deliver him home in time for his son's special day. He would be a very happy man.

Consuelo made sure that Peter was wearing nice pants and a shirt. He kept asking, "Is my daddy coming home today?"

All she could tell him was "We will just have to wait and see. I hope so." She was wishing and hoping—even praying—that he would be there in time. "I will be there in my hospital scrubs in case he is not there. I will see you at two o'clock."

"Oh, Mother, I wanted my daddy to be there!"

"I know, sweetheart."

Her heart was in her mouth when she dropped Peter and Deborah off at the school. It would be a long morning as she waited to hear something from Jeff. She knew he would be there if he could make it.

At 10:30, Consuelo's phone rang. It was Jeff. He was at base operations. He would be at the apartment in a half hour.

She was about to jump out of her skin with excitement. She said, "Peter will be so happy. The teacher will play the video. I will be there in my scrubs. And you can enter and walk up and stand beside Peter. I have it arranged with the principal and teacher. The office staff will give you a visitor's pass. Be sure and wear your flight suit. We can talk more later. Oh, Jeff, I am so excited to see you. It is so good to have you home again. Hurry and get here! Love you."

At 1:30, Consuelo was dressed in hospital scrubs, with name tag and stethoscope. She was ready for the afternoon. Jeff was dressed in flight suit and hat. They left for the school. Jeff would wait until the video was showing when an office aide would bring him into the classroom.

Consuelo was seated with Peter. It was the hardest thing she had ever done not telling Peter that his Daddy was home. Just as the video ended, Jeff quietly walked toward the front of the classroom and started talking about flying the B-2. Peter sat still for a second, then slowly turned his head and saw his daddy standing there looking at him.

He screamed, "Daddy, you made it. You are here. You came. You are home!" He ran and jumped into Jeff's open arms. There were many teary eyes as administrators, teachers, parents, and students witnessed the reunion of a child and his military father.

This Last Mission

Jeff was waiting for Deborah when she came out of her classroom. She was thrilled beyond measure when she saw him. She ran to him, screaming, "Daddy, Daddy, Daddy, you are here!" She wrapped her arms around his neck and buried her face on his shoulder. "Daddy, Daddy, Daddy! I am so glad you are home. I'm never-never-never-ever going to let you go away again!"

After the little family reached the car, the next stop was Ben and Jerry's.

After the promised ice cream treat, they headed to their house for Jeff to see the damage done by an electrical fire. Much of the damage had been cleaned up. The dumpster was full of damaged materials. The storage unit was partially filled with items that had been cleaned or restored. Other pieces of furniture would be added in the days to come.

Jeff was moved emotionally when he saw the damage to the family home. He visited with carpenters and with Carl Hatley. He thanked him for coming with Pastor Johnson and Michael Jameson to meet with the insurance adjustor all those weeks in the past after the fire. The carpenters explained what they would be doing once cleanup was completed. Carl said, "A crew is coming in to clean smoke and soot from the walls, so we can paint the entire house.

"When we are finished, you will have an almost new house. Carpeting must be removed. We have made a lot of progress. Consuelo has pictures of each stage. She wanted you to see what it looked like and what the finished product will look like. Sir, we are happy you are home again." Deborah had one of Jeff's hands and Peter had the other.

Chapter 17

A sort of normality settled in for the little family as they struggled living in a small apartment while the house was being restored.

Consuelo returned to her job. Jeff resumed his normal activities. The children were thrilled to have the family together. It didn't matter to them that they were living in an apartment. Their greatest concern was not having the neighborhood kids to play with.

The months sped by, and soon it was time for summer vacation. Consuelo, Jeff and the children took two weeks of vacation time. They took a road trip out west to visit family. Consuelo's family lived in southwestern Colorado and Jeff's family in southeast Arizona.

The parents planned some fun activities to break up the long car trip: Carlsbad Caverns and the Grand Canyon. When they had seen pictures, videos, and books about it, the children wanted to walk out on the Grand Canyon's famous Skywalk. They were trying to imagine what it would feel like to look through glass and see the canyon hundreds of feet below.

Along the way the parents attempted to stay in motels with swimming pools and children's play equipment. And of course, each child had a traveling entertainment bag. Plus, there was the usual game of counting the red cars, blue cars, etc. The parents attempted to be creative to keep the young children from being bored. Jeff told the children that they could ride horses when they got to his home. He said, "I will teach you how to shoot a bow and arrow. My father will tell you a true story about his grandfather. The story happened when my great-grandfather was a boy. My father is an excellent storyteller."

Consuelo told them about the mountains. "Mother will teach you to make tamales, and my father will teach you how to do the polka. I remember he would always dress in a white shirt and brown lederhosen shorts that had embroidered designs on the suspenders. He would wear white knee socks and a Bavarian felt hat with a feather. You will see the lederhosen he wore when he was a little boy living in Munich, Germany. You will have many things to tell your friends when we get back home."

Excitement was growing.

And best of all, their fire-damaged home should be restored by the time vacation time was over.

Chapter 18

Peter and Deborah were amazed when they walked into the huge gaping hole forming the entrance into Carlsbad Cavern. Each child held tightly to a parent's hand as they descended deeper and deeper into the massive cavern. They saw stalactites and stalagmites on both sides of the passageway. Soon in, a large room, the guide told everyone to stand very still. He wanted the group to experience total darkness. The lights were turned off. Peter and Deborah clung tightly to Jeff and Consuelo. The darkness was so heavy they could almost feel it. Then, the lights were turned on. A big yeah erupted from the happy crowd.

The family exited the entrance and sat in the Bat Flight Amphitheater watching the cavern entrance. Peter exclaimed, "Look! Bats!"

A park ranger was standing nearby. He walked over and sat beside Peter. "My name is Ranger Jack. What is your name?"

Peter looked at his mother and hesitantly said, "Peter."

Ranger Jack said, "Those are Brazilian free-tailed bats. They've been sleeping all day. Now they are going out to get something to eat. They will catch bugs all night. Isn't it exciting to see them? Did you see them fly? Wouldn't you like to fly like that?"

Peter said, "I would rather fly like my daddy."

"Oh? Is your daddy a pilot?"

Proudly Peter responded, "Yes, sir. My daddy flies the B-2 bomber. He can go very fast!"

Ranger Jack turned to Jeff. "Sir, thank you for your service to our country." He stood and saluted Jeff.

This Last Mission

Jeff saluted him back. "Thank you, sir."

Another family called to Ranger Jack. He went to talk with them and stayed in the area answering any question a child or adult might have.

Soon Jeff led his family to the SUV and resumed their journey.

At the visitor's center Consuelo had collected maps, brochures, and other information about Carlsbad for the kid's summer scrapbooks.

Chapter 19

The next day, the family arrived at the Grand Canyon. When the children peeped over the edge of the canyon, they decided they were not interested in standing close to such a big hole in the ground. However, Deborah was thrilled when she walked on to the horseshoe-shaped glass walkway, the Grand Canyon Skywalk. She was excited to look through the glass and see the craggy rocks and cliffs below. A bird flew under the Skywalk, and she squealed with delight.

Jeff said, "She may be the next generation fighter pilot. She is not bothered by heights."

"We will soon arrive at my parents' home in Chinle. Let me remind you about some family history while we drive along. You know your Grandfather Blackhawk and Grand Mama Algoma. But did you know her name means 'Valley of Flowers'? Another piece of family history: my great-grandfather was a code talker in World War II. The Japanese had hacked into the American codes and kept intercepting our messages, which caused us to keep losing battles.

My great-grandfather and other Navajo men were asked to send messages in the Navajo language, and there was no more trouble with hacking into American codes."

Peter said, "You speak Navajo, don't you, Daddy? Oh yes, that's right, I know you do because you have tried to teach me."

"Yes, I do, and maybe we can work harder at teaching you our ancient language when we are home."

This Last Mission

Deborah said, "Daddy, do you have a Navajo name, like Grandfather Blackhawk?"

"Yes, Deborah, my Navajo name is Atsa. Your Uncle Jacob's Navajo name is Bidzil. People in school had so much trouble speaking our names correctly, we assumed the names 'Jeff and Jacob.' Atsa means, Eagle and Bidzil means, very strong."

The family discussed family traditions and old stories as they drove along.

Driving to the family home, Jeff drove by his father's shop. His mechanic shop repaired large engines—diesel trucks, heavy machinery, etc. Jeff and Bidzil worked there when they were in high school and when they were home from college.

Soon they arrived at the family home. Grand Mama Algoma had dinner ready when the weary little family pulled into the driveway. Cousins, nieces and nephews, and uncles and aunts were there. Deborah jumped out of the car and squealed, "Yeah! We are having a party!"

Grand Mama Algoma had long tables set up outside loaded with food. Aunts had brought favorite dishes. There was happy chatter from everyone. Old stories were told, and funny things that had happened in the family were remembered. It was a time of celebrating family.

Soon, it was time for families to return to their homes for the night. Jeff's brother, Jacob invited them to his home in the country the next day. He wanted Peter and Deborah to go horseback riding. Their cousins were saying what fun they would have again tomorrow.

Jeff and Jacob were delighted to have the time together. Jacob wanted to hear about the plane Jeff flies. Soon the brothers were discussing favorite sports and remembering school days, football, and other competitions they had shared.

Peter and Deborah were up early in the morning wanting to go to Uncle Jacob's house. It was another day of family celebrations. Cousins, aunts, uncles and grandparents would spend a day of visiting and playing games, telling old family stories, and enjoying life. For the children, horseback riding was top of the list. They couldn't wait for the horses to be saddled and ready for riding. Deborah and Peter didn't know how to ride but were anxious to have the experience. Older cousins were patient with the two city kids, gently guiding and telling them how to maneuver the reins guiding the horse wherever they wanted him to go. Consuelo took pictures of the entire event. Happily, she had more pictures for the summer vacation photo album.

The following day, Jeff and Jacob taught the children how to shoot bows and arrows. Peter told his big cousin, "You are so lucky to live here. You have horses and can shoot bows and arrows anytime you want to."

Sampson said, "Well, not quiet. We must attend school just like you, and we have chores to do that keeps us busy when we are home. But it is fun when we have the time."

Over dinner, Grand Father Blackhawk announced, "Tomorrow is the last day and night Jeff and family will be with us. In the evening, we will have a family gathering and ceremonial dancing in the circle around a big fire. I will tell the children a story about when my Grandfather was a boy. But tomorrow the braves will be involved in bronco riding and calf-roping.

Meanwhile, Grand Mama Algoma will show the ladies and maidens some of the artwork done by women in our tribe. There is basket weaving, blanket weaving, jewelry making, and pottery. There is more, but I am tired from talking so much."

The big family and friends gathered around the big fire to hear grandfather Blackhawk tell the story about his grandfather. He asked all the children to come and sit on the ground around his feet.

Grandfather Blackhawk began, "My grandfather was Little Rising Star. He was exactly that—little. For all his eleven, almost twelve, years, he would shudder when someone referred to his small size. They just assumed that because he was small, he could not do things as well as the other boys. He knew his loyal friends, Running Buck and Flying Eagle, understood how he felt even though they were much larger than he was. They were there with him and heard the taunts and jeers of the other boys and the uproarious laughter that followed when he failed.

"The other boys loved to 'trash talk.' That group of boys was the tough ones who were always creating trouble. They were bullies.

"He promised himself that one day he would show the villagers that size wasn't everything. He would do something very important and then they would see!

"Spring would soon reach the mountain range, where Little Rising Star and his tribe lived. Winter, with its drab, grey skies, bone-chilling winds, and snowstorms would soon weaken its grip, giving away to slightly milder spring weather. Then, as weak rays of sunshine reached the forests, tiny buds would begin to form on trees as tiny tips of green leaves began to show. Before winter's end, just before spring arrived in the mountains, young braves were given tests of bravery. They were tested on events of strength and bravery. There was bareback horseback riding and other tests of quickness and strength. They competed with bows and arrows. There were knife skills every brave young man needed to know.

"Because the other boys were much taller and stronger than Little Riding Star, he usually finished last in most events, except when he was using his bow and arrow.

"In the big competition for test of bravery, they would compete with one another. Each one would go alone, on his own. He would have a backpack with food. He would get water from clear, cold, rushing streams in the mountains. The tests of bravery were such that the boys had to travel, on foot, over mountain trails, and across roaring rivers and creeks. They had to climb treacherous cliffs, kill an animal, and return to the village.

"The boys knew that Old One Eye, a ferocious lone grey wolf with blood-curdling howls, lurked in the mountains. Old One Eye had roamed the mountains for many years. Prickles of fear ran up Little Rising Star's back as he remembered the legend of the lone grey wolf.

Old One Eye, whose scarred face and tattered and torn ears, and the vacant place where an eye once was, were all reminders of his years of fighting with other wolves. The legends said that Old One Eye was an evil spirit that had come back to the mountains to capture young braves and beautiful Indian maidens.

"Little Rising Star had begun strength building and exercise as he trained during the harsh winter months. Day after day he trained until his muscles ached from running and climbing. His hands were raw from practicing with bow and arrow and using his knife to cut small tree limbs for fire.

"Finally, the long-awaited day arrived. The first event was bareback riding. There were many beautiful horses, including Little Rising Star's spirited pony, a brown and white paint.

"Flying Eagle had a powerful black horse with four white feet. Running Buck's was a frisky chestnut brown horse. From the first hoof beat, Running Buck's horse was in the lead, and Little Rising Star's little paint pony came in last place. Little Rising Star swallowed hard, attempting to stand strong after experiencing another defeat.

"On the day they were to go on their adventure, each young brave was to carry a backpack along with bows and arrows. The families lined the ceremonial grounds as their sons were given instructions for competition. As a sign of bravery each was to bring home an animal they had killed.

"The group of young braves was lined up and walking together as they left the village. Soon the stronger distanced themselves from the slower boys.

"Little Rising Star could see clouds looming over the mountains. He could hear thunder and see lightning bolts cut across the sky and feel icy blasts of wind. He had been taught to read the signs of weather. He knew winter was weakening but was not over. He would soon seek shelter before night. He would need to gather dry limbs and twigs, cut limbs from trees and build a fire. He hoped he could find a small cave to get inside so he would be out of the icy wind.

"The mountain trails on which he was walking were icy and dangerous. He knew that if he stepped wrong on the slippery rocks, he could fall a long way down the mountainside. There were icy patches on the trails, and he could see snow packed in crevasses in the rocks. Little Rising Star kept trudging along. His training was paying off; his muscles were taut and strong. His heart leaped in his chest as he passed boys who had been in the lead group. Steadily he climbed the steep mountainsides. From that height he could look down into the valley far below.

"He had not seen any of the other boys in two or three days. The test of bravery was about to draw to an end.

"As he cautiously walked along the slippery, rocky ledge on the mountainside, he was startled to see rocks crashing down from above. As the rocks came down, they broke small trees, then fell down the mountainside. Alarmed squirrels were chattering and scampering out of the way. Just as the rock side was ending and only small rocks and dirt were sliding down, Little Rising Star heard a sickening thud. It didn't sound like rocks or tree limbs. He peeked around a large rock wall he had hidden behind when the rockslide began to see what the different sound might be. The prickle of fear caused the hair to stand up on the back of his neck when he saw Running Buck lying on a wider part of the ledge. He had fallen! Then, Little Rising Star saw Old One Eye stealthily approaching Running Buck.

"Quick as lightning, Little Rising Star's hand shot up to his quiver and plucked out an arrow. Instantly, bow and arrow met. The arrow sped toward its target. The point of the arrow sank deep into Old One Eye's heart. The large grey wolf lay crumpled beside bleeding, dazed and terrified Running Buck.

"With knees shaking and hearts racing, the two friends exchanged thankful greetings. Little Rising Star stood frozen to the ground as he looked in awe at the once greatly feared lone grey wolf. His mind jerked him back to reality; he had to care for his injured friend.

"Running Buck had deep cuts on his head and on his leg. His body, legs, and arms had no broken bones, just scrapes, cuts, and bruises.

"Little Rising Star used scraps of cloth and sphagnum moss with which to bind up the gashes on his friend's head and leg.

"Earlier in the day, when he was in a meadow, he had killed a rabbit for his evening meal. After getting Running Buck into an outcropping of rock that formed a shelter from wind and rain, Little Rising Star gathered sticks, twigs, and limbs from trees to build a fire. He also cut live saplings to form a rack to cook the rabbit over the fire. Not only would the fire keep them warm, but they could cook the rabbit. Most importantly, wild animals do not like fire, so the fire would help keep the two boys safe during the long, cold night. Last of all, he moved Old One Eye's body out of the way.

"The two friends had talked far into the night telling stories of their first journey. During the night, a fierce storm passed over the mountains, but the two friends were dry and warm.

"The next morning Little Rising Star fashioned a litter by using two long poles and rawhide strips of leather. He suspended Old One Eye's body between the poles, tying it securely with rawhide strips. With the two poles resting on his shoulders Little Rising Star began to pull the litter, while Running Buck, bruised, scraped, cut, and sore, limped alongside him. Running Buck was a strong young brave, so there was never a whimper about how bad he was hurting. He was a brave, and braves are strong!

"When they entered the village, Running Buck related the story of how little Rising Star had saved his life by killing the feared grey wolf. That night, at the ceremonial grounds and fire celebration, Little Rising Star was declared the bravest of all. As a symbol of his bravery, the chief promised to give Little Rising Star a necklace made of Old One Eye's teeth, and his pelt would be made into a warm jacket for the cold winter months.

"Suddenly, little didn't sound bad at all. In fact, he liked it, because he liked himself just the way he was! He realized it is not the size of a person that matters; it is what is in the heart."

Grandfather Blackhawk continued, "Children, you see this necklace I am wearing? This necklace was made of old One Eye's teeth. This belonged to my grandfather. The moral of the story: Just because a lot of kids may be larger or more skilled than you, do not give up. It is not the size of the person that counts. It is the determination in the heart that makes a brave—or an Indian princess."

Other boys and girls and young people from the community had come to sit around the large fire and hear the story. They had heard it many times before. Grand Father Blackhawk was an excellent storyteller, and everyone loved to hear his deep voice telling the story. Everyone clapped their hands and said in unison, "Thank you, Grand Father Blackhawk."

"My son and family, we will miss you when you go on your big journey to your next destination. We are thankful to have Jacob and his family close by, yet we always miss the ones who are not sitting around our community fire. We will once again welcome the day when Jeff and family return to our village next summer."

Chapter 20

After breakfast, Jeff and family loaded into the SUV and began the trip to Durango. Everyone was sad to be leaving Grand Father Blackhawk and Grand Mama Algoma. As they drove away, they waved goodbye. They all said, "We will see you next summer."

Peter said, "It is hard being a military kid. We miss being with family."

Deborah said, "Yes, but if we lived here, we couldn't have Chunky Monkey ice cream." That made everyone laugh.

Consuelo said, "Remember, my mother is Mexican, and my father is from Germany. Grandmother is Abuela, and grandfather is Opa. Repeat it with me, just as a refresher. Abuela will show us many things from her culture. We will have a fiesta tonight. There will be a mariachi band, dancers in beautiful costumes, and lots of music. Tomorrow, Opa will dress in lederhosen, a white shirt, and a hat with a feather in it. He will dance for you as he did when he was a boy in Germany. Tomorrow the family will make tamales. It is fun when we all make them together."

The hours flew by, and soon they arrived in Abuela and Opa's driveway. Consuelo's four brothers and three sisters were there, as well as many nieces and nephews. Peter and Deborah had forgotten what a large family was waiting for them. A piñata was hanging in a tree in the backyard. Abuela said it was for breaking later, not now. Strings of party lights were strung around the patio. Tables were set up for tons of food the family had brought for the meal.

This Last Mission

Everyone was talking over the next person and the volume grew louder and louder. People were laughing, while kids were playing ball and yelling to make themselves heard. Consuelo said to her daddy, "It is a good thing you have a big backyard to hold all these kids!"

"My Chiquita, it is good to have you home. We look forward all year to when you and the family can come home for a few days. Your little ones are growing up so fast. Enjoy them while you can. Childhood passes much too quickly. It seems you and your brothers and sisters should be that size rather than having families of your own." He sighed deeply. "Yes, Chiquita. Life goes by much too quickly. There is something I must tell you. Uh oh, your wonderful mother is trying to get everyone's attention. I better help her." He gave a shrill whistle that stopped everyone in their tracks!

Abuela said, "Dinner is ready. Wash your hands and get to the table."

Tables were set up on the tree-covered patio. Dusk was falling, party lights were turned on, and candles were lit on each table.

Everyone became quiet while Opa gave thanks to God for the food, for traveling mercy, for everyone coming, and for bringing Consuelo and her family safely home from a long drive across the country. He added, "And, thank you our Father in heaven for all these children! Amen."

Happy chatter resumed. When the meal was ending, some of the family quietly left the table, only to return a few minutes later. Ladies were dressed in colorful dresses and men in black pants, white shirts, and sombreros. A mariachi band began playing and strolling around the tables. At one side of the patio dancers began taking their positions. Ladies with castanets began dancing. There were whistles and clapping, and someone yelled, "Arriba, arriba!"

A festive evening was soon in progress.

Deborah asked, "Mommy, can you dance like that?"

Opa heard her question and answered, "Mi nieta, Consuelo dances beautifully. Yes, she can do all these dances. But tonight, she is a guest of honor. They are dancing for her. I will show you pictures of her dancing. Remind me tomorrow and we will look at photo albums."

Chapter 21

The next day was spent viewing old pictures, making tamales, and, after another family dinner, breaking the piñata. During all the noisy celebration, Jeff's phone rang. He went to one side to answer it. Consuelo was curious who might be calling and watched to see his reaction. He seemed to freeze for a moment, then turned and looked at her, then at the family. She knew without a word being spoken. She went to him and he engulfed her in his arms. Neither said a word for several minutes. Finally, she asked, "When do they want you to return home?"

"As soon as I can get back home. I will be packing for an indefinite period. Things are getting hot again."

"Where will you fly out for home base?"

"I am to be at Peterson AFB in Colorado Springs tomorrow afternoon to catch a C-130 heading back to our home base. I hate to leave you and the children to travel alone back across country. I wish you would be there waiting for me when I get back home."

"Don't worry; we will be fine. We won't have as good of a time as when you are there with us, but we will make it. I better go get to packing. We need to get on the road as soon as we can."

"But first we must tell the family," Jeff said.

Tears were flowing as family lined up to say goodbye. Consuelo, attempting to sound brave, said with a breaking voice, "We knew this was a possibility. We just hoped it wouldn't happen. Pray for us all."

This Last Mission

Hugs and kisses were given as the little family loaded into the SUV and headed toward Colorado Springs. No one spoke for several minutes. Then Deborah said, "Daddy, I wished you wouldn't have to go. We like having you home with us."

Jeff's face flushed. He kept swallowing and swallowing, attempting to gain control of his voice. Eventually he said, "Little princess, I like being home. This is just my job. Soon I will be coming back home again. Then we can go get another Chunky Monkey. Is that okay?"

Peter spoke up. "It is okay, but it is not all right. We will miss you."

Consuelo was doing her best to hold herself together and not make matters worse for Jeff. Fortunately, the heavy moment was broken when they saw a man attempting to lead a little donkey down the road. However, the donkey didn't want to go that direction, so he sat down. The man was pulling and pushing on the stubborn animal. The donkey had his ears back, not looking happy, as the man tugged and pulled on the rope and then flopped his big hat against the donkey's rump. The man's face was angry, and he was saying something to the donkey, but the family couldn't hear what was said. Jeff slowed down to watch what would happen next. The family was laughing heartily at the sight they were witnessing.

The rest of the drive to Colorado Springs, someone would start laughing and the other three would join in the happy memory.

The next morning, the little family had a leisurely breakfast, then it was time to take Jeff to the base. Four individuals with very heavy hearts said their goodbyes. Consuelo and the children watched Jeff walk away and disappear into a building. Slowly, Consuelo drove the car off the base and headed for home. She was wiping tears and the children were comforting one another.

So, goes the life of a military family. It doesn't matter which branch of service or rank. Goodbyes to the ones you love never become easy.

Chapter 22

Consuelo had driven to downtown Denver, so the children could see the golden dome on the state capitol building. After they left the city and were heading east, the children were entertaining themselves with their travel packages and Consuelo was deep in thought. As they rounded a corner, she saw debris scattered across the highway and a loaded junk truck on ahead. Consuelo hit the brakes in an attempt to dodge as much debris as she could, but she hit a large piece of metal, which caught the left front tire and fender. She swerved across the road and managed to keep her vehicle upright, stopping along a guardrail. Just ahead of her, two cars and truck collided, smashing into the guardrail. Two more cars slid into them. Screeching tires were heard as the other vehicles were wrecked. Another car came careening past Consuelo and crashed just ahead of her car.

Consuelo called 911, reporting numerous cars in a pileup east of Denver. She gave the mileage marker, and she added, "I am a nurse practitioner. I want to go to see how I may help, but I can't leave my small children in the car."

The operator said, "Do not leave your children unattended. Remain in your vehicle. It is too dangerous for you to exit the vehicle. Help is on the way." He kept asking question after question. "How many vehicles can you see from where you are located? Are there any fires?"

She responded, "I can see six or eight vehicles in front of me and several behind me. There are no fires that I can see. Victims are helping one another out of smashed vehicles. Some victims are lying on the highway. I see several head wounds. I feel I need to go help. I have

This Last Mission

a medical kit with me and could begin triage while ambulances are coming…but my children. You better send several ambulances. There are a lot of injuries."

The operator asked, "What caused the accidents?"

She responded quickly, "There was debris all across the road. A large piece of metal struck my left fender and punctured my left tire. Ahead of us, a junk truck was carrying a load of trash; some of it fell off the moving vehicle. Sir, please hurry. Their people are in bad shape."

Consuelo screamed, "Children, put your heads down. A car is going to hit us!"

There was the sound of screeching tires and a loud, jolting crash. Grating steel and shattering glass. The children were screaming.

The operator shouted, "Ma'am, ma'am, are you alright? How are your children?"

Frantic sounds could be heard by the operator as he listened helplessly as a mother was attempting to comfort her terrified children. They were all crying.

Sobbing, Consuelo said, "A car slid into our car. The front of his car is against the guardrail, and the side of the car has caved in the back of my SUV and deployed the airbags. My children and I are okay. Sir, I cannot see inside the other vehicle. I do not see anyone moving."

The operator was shaken by what he had heard. He resumed talking in a calm voice and tried to direct her thoughts away from the terror they had just experienced.

He said, "How old are your children?"

"One is five, and the other one just celebrated his seventh birthday."

"Absolutely, I agree with you, stay in that vehicle! Keep talking to me. Where were you heading when this happened?"

Through her tears, she said, "We had been on vacation, and my husband was called back to work. I had dropped him off at Peterson AFB to catch a plane back to his home base. He is being deployed. The children and I are on our way home. We live in another state."

"Your husband is military? What does he do?"

"He is a B-2 pilot. Sir, I can see emergency vehicles approaching."

"Good. That is what I was waiting to hear. I know you are shaken up. Are you better? They know about your medical skills. Do you think you can help with the injured? Someone will be staying with your children. You are requested to help the EMS. Stay in your vehicle until someone approaches you. They will bring a policewoman to keep your children. Good luck to you and your family. I am sorry for what you have experienced today. Goodbye."

A highway patrolman was knocking on her window. She rolled down the window, and he said, "Officer Whiteman will be staying with your children. Grab your medical bag and let's get going. There are injured people everywhere. There are more vehicles behind us with injuries."

"I'll have to climb over into the back seat and see if I can get my bag. The car behind me has rendered the back of my SUV useless."

Consuelo told the children that she would be helping some people who were hurt very badly and for them to be good for the police lady.

Late that afternoon, the last emergency vehicle pulled away and a policeman changed Consuelo's tire. He said, "Your vehicle is badly damaged but drivable. If you promise me that you will take it to a dealer just as soon as you get home, I will release you." She and the children headed on their journey. It was a struggle, but she could drive the badly damaged vehicle.

When they entered a small town, they located a motel and stopped for the night. Once inside the building, she called Jeff. She was hoping he was safely back home and getting packed.

Jeff answered the phone. He was in their apartment. He had driven by the house. It was almost finished. Then he asked how her day had gone. He was not prepared for the answer. He was startled to hear of a multi-car pileup. She had helped with the injured. A policewoman stayed with the children while she helped care for the injured victims.

Jeff said he would be leaving the next day. "It appears we may not be gone as long this time. Hopefully, it appears I will be back in time to help you move back into the house."

This Last Mission

Peter wanted to talk with his Daddy. He said, "Daddy, there were wrecked cars everywhere. A car hit us too. Lots of people were hurt badly. Momma helped them while Officer Whiteman stayed with us. She was a nice lady. Deborah is about to have a fit because she wants to talk with you. Daddy, sometimes this girl drives me crazy!"

"Daddy, a truck was in front of us, and he dropped big pieces of stuff all over the road. Cars hit it and got wrecked. Daddy, I was scared, and I cried. I miss you, Daddy. I want to be a police lady when I grow up, just like Officer Whiteman. She is nice. Love you, Daddy. Bye. Here is Mommy."

Consuelo laughed. "I guess she said all she needed to say."

Laughing, Jeff replied, "I had to listen fast. I hope I understood. With that girl, you only get one chance to catch the message.

"Changing the subject. Jolene and Bill are divorcing. As soon as the divorce is final, she is moving back to her hometown in Virginia. The word around the squadron is he is retiring. He said he will be flying for commercial airlines. He has already applied with several airlines."

"Before Jolene was admitted to the hospital, she told me she had filed for a divorce. He has been living elsewhere for some time," Consuelo said.

"When do you think you and the kids will be home?"

"Two or three days. It depends on the SUV. It is really banged up. Will you please call the insurance company? It was a bit hectic at the accident site. Tell them the left front fender is smashed and the trunk area is caved in. I'll take pictures and send them to you. You can forward them to the company. I'll give them the location, highway patrol officer's number, etc. I have it all. Anyway, I do not make as good time as when you are driving, especially with a vehicle that is this damaged, but we will be home soon. When you reach Guam, give me a call so I will know you are there safely. Oh yes, Peter remembered that Opa had told him he would show him how to do a German dance and would wear his lederhosen, but we ran out of time. That reminds me, Daddy said he had something he needed to discuss with me. I just remembered. Hum, I wonder what it was."

Jeff said, "I hate to cut this short, but I need to go to bed. I have to get up at 3:00 a.m. and go to the base for my flight west. I am thankful you are all right. I will call the insurance company. Send those pictures. I love and miss you. We will be together soon. Love you."

"I love you too and miss you." Consuelo was batting back tears as she signed off for the night.

Chapter 23

Eventually, three very weary travelers arrived back at the apartment. They fell happily into their own beds. And happily, they did not have to roll out of bed for another day of travel.

Consuelo's next responsibility was to take the SUV to a body shop for repairs. The insurance company had contacted her and would have a representative at the apartment the next day.

She would be without her car for a lengthy period of time. That would mean driving a loaner vehicle for a few days. She thought, when will life gets back to normal? Will I even recognize normal when it comes along? A rental car? Living in an apartment? Needing to buy new furniture? Move back in the house? Ugh!

Consuelo contacted her office and gave a report that she was back in town earlier than expected. She recounted all the events of the past several days. She said, "The kids start summer camp next week, and I will be back at work. It will feel good to have a normal routine. The house is almost finished. I just hope Jeff will be back home when it is time to move in. Next task is to purchase appliances and new living room furniture. Life has been crazy lately! I am looking forward to normal. See you Monday."

Gerry called and left a message. "There is to be a tea tomorrow. Do you think you can come? We will be saying goodbye to some of our friends who are transferring to other bases and welcoming new people.

There is a lot you and I need to catch up on. My husband said you had a rough trip home. Call me."

Consuelo squeezed in time to go to the tea. She had an appointment to drop off the heavily damaged SUV later in the day. Needless to say, her vehicle was the center of attention in front of the host's home.

Jolene was at the tea. She gave Consuelo a big hug and thanked her for all the phone calls and visits. She promised to keep in touch.

Several couples were transferring to other bases. It was a "hail and farewell" tea. Consuelo was happy she could meet the new people. As she was saying farewell to old friends, one of them said, "Consuelo, you and Jeff have been here, what, four years? Aren't you guys due to transfer?"

When she heard that, Consuelo had a stricken expression on her face at the thought of packing up and moving again after all their family had been through the past few months. She was speechless. After a lengthy pause, she said, "At the moment, I shudder at the thought of moving."

Consuelo looked at her watch and saw the time was approaching when the SUV would need to be at the shop. She thanked the hostess and said bye to Gerry and dashed out the door. Peter and Deborah had spent the afternoon with their neighborhood friends. Consuelo was feeling pressure to go get them as soon as she could. But first, she had to deal with the body shop and get a rental or loaner vehicle.

When the insurance adjuster saw the SUV, he said, "Where were you when you were in the accident?"

Consuelo recounted the accident and how she had limped along across country in the damaged vehicle.

In shock, he said, "Please tell me you didn't drive that far in this vehicle? I am surprised you made it home. No pun intended, but this thing is a wreck! When that car slid into the back of your SUV with such force, he caught the left fender area as well as crashing into the back of the vehicle. The frame is bent. The entire left side of the SUV would need to be replaced. I am saying this vehicle is totaled. Lady, I do not know how you made it back home. This vehicle must have looked weird driving forward, the back wheels were making one set of tire marks and the front wheels another. To be blunt, you were driving a death trap. I am calling a tow truck to haul it away. Get all valuables out immediately—car seats, papers, everything."

"What will I do for transportation? Will your company provide a rental?"

"Yes, that is included in your coverage. I will fill out the paperwork and let me hear from you when you purchase your next vehicle. We will be happy to take care of your new mode of transportation."

When Consuelo thought she might have a chance of making a connection with Jeff, she called him. Fortunately, he was not flying. She gave a full accounting of what the insurance adjuster had said, that the vehicle was totaled. She said, "Now my next challenge is to get a rental vehicle until we can purchase a car. I am hoping I can delay that purchase until you are home and can help make that decision. I am thankful we live in this period in history when we have cell phones and computers. My grandmother said when she and Grandpa were in the military, they didn't hear from each other for days or weeks. They got their messages through an occasional letter, another military guy, or a ham operator. My grandmother had to make all the decisions alone. Jeff, you are not here, but at least I can talk with you, and that means a lot. It helps to have your encouragement. How did they stay together? We think it is hard now. It must have been awful for them. The families didn't know when their husbands/fathers would be back, and in many cases, they had no way of knowing."

Deborah came in the room, where Consuelo was talking to Jeff. She yelled, "Peter, Mommy is talking with Daddy and I am first getting to talk with Daddy tonight ... Naa-naa-naa- naa-boo-boo...."

Consuelo said, "Just one-minute, young lady, and I will give you the phone. Anyway, that was not a nice way to talk with your brother! Jeff, it looks like the phone has been commandeered by a short person." In a dramatic tone of voice, she said, "And here is Deborah!"

"Hi, Daddy. Today we got to play with our friends. It's been a long time since we got to play. They have a new puppy. Daddy, can I have a new puppy? They have a Saint Bernard puppy. Oh, Daddy, will you bring me a Saint Bernard puppy on the airplane? Here is Peter. Love you, Daddy. Bye."

Calmly Peter took the phone. In a dignified tone of voice, he said, "You know, Daddy, that girl is driving me crazy! I sure do want to see you. I need to have another man in this house. I hope you will come home soon. I miss you. Here is Mama."

Jeff was laughing when she retrieved the phone. He said, "What will that girl want me to bring her 'on my airplane' next? Peter must feel like he gets steamrolled by her every day. She is a bundle of energy! I suppose I should laugh at it; after all, I am half a world away from all the action. Sometimes I think you are the one who should be getting metals and ribbons. Okay, as for the car, go back to the dealer when the insurance check comes in. I'll ask Colonel Harrison if one of the guys will go with you to bargain with the dealer. I understand a man can get a better deal than a woman can. Sorry, sweetie, but women are viewed as soft or weak and not savvy enough in business matters to deal with a car dealer. But do your research. Know what you want in a vehicle. Make up your mind how much you want to pay, and don't pay a dollar over that price. Don't let the salesperson bully you. Tell the salesperson your expectations and walk out if they are not willing to negotiate. Stand your ground with him or her."

Consuelo was all fired up. "Well! If I am so soft and weak, I would like to see him or her deal with what I have dealt with the past few months. Then let's see who is soft!"

Jeff was laughing his sides out. Teasingly he said, "Go get 'em tiger! You've got what it takes. They don't know what is waiting for them. You can do this." He continued laughing.

She said, "Oh you! Stop laughing at me!" She was soon laughing too. "Jeff, I miss you so much. I can't wait for you to come home."

"I think I will be home in two weeks, maybe sooner. I'll let you know as soon as I know. Oh yes, not sure this is a good time to tell you this, but we may have a transfer coming up in the next six months to a year. We will talk about that when I get home. Love you and will see you soon."

"Whoa! Wait a minute! What did you just say? Where? When?"

"Not sure I can answer that many questions on a half of a cell phone battery. There are a couple of possibilities. Nothing is firmed up. I understand the B-2 may be phased out at our base and another craft will be replacing it. So right now, there is a lot of speculation including, I may be checked out in the new aircraft. Then again, it may be a squadron transfer. We'll see. There are lots of possibilities. I'll tell you more as I know more. I really must go this time. Love you."

Chapter 24

Consuelo was at work when her phone rang. She couldn't take the call but noticed it was from the contractor. As soon as she finished with the patient, she would call him back.

Eventually she returned the phone call. Mr. Hatley said, "Consuelo, we are waiting for inspectors to sign off on the job. We have been waiting on them for about two weeks. They must check off everything we have done, and it must be up to code before we can complete the job. I thought you needed to know what is holding up the process. As soon as they do their job, we will finish ours. Have a good afternoon."

Consuelo held the phone in her hand and mumbled, "I could write a book about the past eight months!"

As she was standing deep in thought, a nurse ran into the room and said, "There is an emergency in room number seven. Hurry. One of your patients collapsed getting onto the examining table."

Two nurses were attending him. Consuelo knelt down beside him and said, "Hello, Mr. Jones, what happened? Do you know who I am?" She began the examination as she asked the nurses to attach the EKG machine.

Mr. Jones weakly nodded his head. "Good. Can you talk to me? We are taking care of you. We will have you feeling better. Hold on. Just try to relax."

Consuelo said, "Call Dr. Gutierrez. Hurry! He was going to the hospital." Consuelo began the examination. She said, "Tell him it looks like Mr. Jones may have had a heart attack. Call 911." She began working on the overweight man. He was lying in the floor.

This Last Mission

She said, "Mr. Jones, Doctors Swarovski and Hielaman are here. Just try to relax. An ambulance will soon be here. We will take you to the heart hospital. They have more equipment than we have in this office. Soon the ambulance will arrive, and they will transport you to the hospital."

The doctors were working frantically over the patient. An IV was started and medication was administered. Mr. Jones was holding tightly to Consuelo's hand. He said, "Will you ride with me to the hospital? My wife is dead, and I have no one. Please stay with me."

Consuelo said, "Yes, Mr. Jones I will go with you. Dr. Gutierrez will be at the hospital waiting for us."

The doctors exchanged looks and they glanced at the nurses. They all knew that her military husband was in Guam and there was no one to pick up her children from summer camp.

One of the nurses whispered, "Don't worry about your children. I will pick them up.

"They can stay with me until you get home."

At the hospital, Dr. Gutierrez was examining Mr. Jones. "I think we have some good news for you," he said. "You did have a slight heart attack. The good news is you were in our office when it happened and could receive immediate care. The bad news is you've got to get some of this weight off. Roger, you and I go back a long way, since before your wife died. We've had these talks before. This time I am very serious. You must stop with the buttered popcorn, sodas, and junk food you eat while watching TV. You must get more exercise!"

Mr. Jones looked at Consuelo and said, "Help me! He is taking away my favorite food! Don't let him do this to me."

"Now, Mr. Jones. I would like to help you, so I will."

Dr. Gutierrez's head popped up and said, "You will do what? Now don't work against me with our patient." He looked at Consuelo and winked.

"Yes, sir. I will have you come into the office every two weeks to be weighed. There is a good dietician in our building who will help you to learn to eat healthier. We will be a team. Mr. Jones, you can do this. Pretty soon you will be so lean and healthy that the widow down the street from you will be knocking on your door."

"Oh, Consuelo. I thought you were my friend. A diet? Me? Really? At my age? Hmm, come to think of it, it would be nice to have some female companionship. Maybe I will try this dietician and see what she suggests. She better not tell me, 'No ice cream, no fried food, or no salt,' or the deal will be off!" With a scowl on his face, he crossed his arms in a defiant manner.

With a shrug of her shoulders, Consuelo said, "Suit yourself. That good-looking widow may get tired of waiting for you and go looking for another guy who is lean, healthy, and fun and just leave you sitting on the sofa with a bowl of buttered popcorn and the TV. That TV is a pretty lonely piece of equipment, if you ask me. I would think the widow woman might be a lot more exciting."

Dr. Gutierrez burst out laughing and so did Mr. Jones. He said, "Roger, give it up. You know better than to argue with a woman, especially when she is right."

"Okay Doc, if you say so."

"We will keep you here in the hospital for a couple of days to see how you do. If you do fine, then we will let you go home. One or the other of us will be checking in on you. And there is a doctor here who will also watch over you if you have a need. Consuelo, are you ready to go home?"

"Oh, Consuelo, I forgot to ask you, how is that handsome husband of yours? Is he home?"

"Thank you for asking about him. Jeff was fine the last time I talked with him. No, he is not home. He is away on a mission. He may be coming home soon. I hope so anyway."

"Well, what are you doing here at this hospital with me? You have children at home who need you. Get a-going! They need you. Thanks for taking care of me while this doctor was out running around on business."

"Bye, Mr. Jones, I hope to be here tomorrow. One or the other of us will be here. Rest well."

Turning to Dr. Gutierrez, Consuelo asked, "Can you give me a lift back to the office? My car is there. I rode to the hospital with Mr. Jones in the ambulance."

CHAPTER 25

"I hope to be home in a week so long as no crises arise in the meantime," Jeff said.

Consuelo was overjoyed to hear his voice. She tried to bring him up to date on the builder's message about waiting for inspection to be completed. And of course, to tell him about Mr. Jones's health issue. She added, "Jeff, he is such a dear old man. You would love to meet him."

Peter and Deborah each had to take their turns telling about their experiences at day camp. Peter told about climbing the rock wall. Deborah caught a fish.

She said, "Daddy, I wanted to put it in my backpack and save it to show you when you come home, but they made me put it back in the water. I cried."

The week sped by and the weekend soon arrived. The little family was found in their usual seats at church. Consuelo bowed her head and prayed that God would give her strength to care for her family. She asked God to protect Jeff and bring him safely home.

The pastor's message, "A Brief Glimpse into Heaven," used a scripture from the New International Version, 1 John 3:1:

How great is love the Father has lavished on us, that we should be called children of God! And that is what we are! The reason the world does not know us is that it did not know him. Dear friends, now we are children of God, and what we will be has not yet been made known. But we know that when Christ appears, we shall be like him, for we shall see him as he is. All who have this hope in him purify themselves, just as he is pure.

He discussed how those who believe on the Lord Jesus Christ will one day have a new body and will live forever in the beautiful kingdom that God has prepared as described in Revelation 21. There will be streets of gold, gates of pearls, and jewels of every color and description in layers upon layers.

As she meditated on the point, he told about no more goodbyes for believers in Jesus, Consuelo wiped away tears from her eyes. Painful loneliness swept over her. She missed Jeff. The pastor continued, "Brothers and sisters, there will be no more heartache, sickness, tears, or sadness. For eternity we will be in the presence of God."

Such hope and promise lifted Consuelo's spirit. Soon the final song, "I Can Only Imagine," was sung by a soloist, and the last prayer of blessing, hope, and protection was said.

Driving home, Peter asked, "Can we go someplace fun to eat? Can we do something different for lunch today?"

"That sounds like a good idea. What did you have in mind?"

The discussion went on and on. Deborah just wanted ice cream and hot dogs. In the middle of the discussion, the phone rang. Consuelo clicked on to the hands-free device and said, "Hello?"

It was Jeff!

"Where are you guys?"

There were all sorts of squealing and yells of "Hi, Daddy!" from the kids. Excitedly Consuelo said, "The question is, where are you? There is no echo. It sounds like you are right here."

"Well, that is because I am! I decided to surprise you and come home a couple of days early. Can you meet me at City Café? Then after lunch, we can go get Chunky Monkeys for anyone interested."

The kids were clapping their hands and saying, "Yeah! Daddy is home. Daddy is home!" When they pulled in to the parking lot, Jeff was standing by the door waiting for them. The children ran across the parking lot to greet their daddy. Consuelo was yelling, "Watch out for cars!" She was hurrying to him as quickly as she could. He was holding a child in each arm. They were hugging him and talking a mile a minute. He was laughing and then slid each little one to the ground and engulfed Consuelo in his arms. Several people were watching.

An older man said, "Are you just returning from assignment?"

Jeff replied, "Yes, I have been away several weeks."

The older man said "I thought so. I was in the Vietnamese conflict, and I remember coming home to my family. The public has no idea what goes on in family life for military families. I was in for twenty-seven years … medial retirement. How long have you been serving?"

"Counting Air Force Academy years, I have been in fifteen years." The conversation continued as Jeff and family and the older man and his wife entered the restaurant. They shook hands and patted each other on the back. A strong military bond reached across generations.

Once seated in a booth, Jeff and Consuelo were facing one direction and the children were facing them. A television was directly in front of the couple. The family was chatting happily when there was a newsflash on the TV screen. Both parents shushed the children and said, "What is this?"

The reporter said, "The Pentagon has just released a video showing an encounter between a B-2 bomber and two Russian fighter planes. The fighters were buzzing the bomber and appeared to be attempting to force the American plane to fly out of international airspace and into an area where they could do a shoot down. The B-2 accelerated his speed and climbed to an altitude of 48,000 feet and then returned safely to base. Several Navy fighter planes joined in fending off the aggressors, which soon discouraged the Russian harassment. The Russian fighter planes dropped out of the pursuit."

Wide-eyed with tears streaming down her face, Consuelo looked at Jeff. Their eyes met. He simply nodded his head. He said, "I wanted to tell you about it, but I see the media has done it for me." He gently wiped the tears from her cheeks and held her in his arms.

There was a tap on Jeff's shoulder. It was the old Vietnam military guy. He said, "Son, I was watching you two when that video came on. I

This Last Mission

was a fighter pilot in the Vietnamese war. That was you, wasn't it! Good flying, young man. I am glad you made it home safely. By the way, son, what rank are you?" "I am a major, sir and you?"

The older man said, "I retired as a bird colonel. God bless you, son. You will go far."

The two men saluted. Then he turned and walked back to his table, where his wife was patiently waiting for him. She was looking up at him. He nodded. She smiled and reached for his hand.

Chapter 26

The next weeks sped by. The little family moved back into their newly restored home. The children had returned to school and life seemed to return to a sense of normalcy.

Consuelo was at work when her phone rang. She glanced at the number and saw it was her parents' home phone number. She told the nurse, "I must take this call. Will you stay with the patient? I shouldn't be gone long. When she answered the call, it was her mother. In anguish, she said, "Consuelo. It is your daddy. He is in the hospital. He has had a stroke. The doctor said that it doesn't look good. Can you come home?"

With her mind in a buzz, Consuelo finished with the patient and then talked with the head of the clinic, Dr. Gutierrez, and explained the situation.

He said, "Consuelo, you are an excellent NP, and I value you very much. Your patients love you, and you love your job, and I appreciate having you on my staff. However, you have had to be away from your position far too much. I am afraid we will need to find another person to fill your spot permanently. Go. Take care of your family matters. We will talk when you return."

Consuelo called Jeff and relayed the information about her dad and about her job situation and said, "I must go home, Jeff."

He said, "Of course. The kids and I will be just fine. Do you want me to make flight reservations for you? Are you still at work?"

This Last Mission

Consuelo took a red-eye special into Durango, Colorado. Rimando, one of her brothers, was there to meet her. He brought her up to date on their dad. He had not gained consciousness. Their mother had not left his side.

As they entered the floor where their dad was hospitalized, Consuelo stopped by the nurse's station and gave her name, that she was an NP, and daughter of Abelard Müller. She explained that she would like to see his file. She was also his medical power of attorney. The nurse handed her the file. She scanned the data. Her face turned pale when she read, "Massive stroke, no brain waves detected." Then they walked into the hospital room. The entire family was there. Consuelo made her way to his bedside. She hugged her mother and held her daddy's limp hand. It was a very emotional moment for everyone. The entire family was there to make a painful decision.

Jeff and the children flew out for the funeral. Consuelo's siblings lived in and around Durango and would be there to assist Abuela with all the final business affairs. After a few days Jeff, Consuelo and children flew home.

Consuelo went back to work and talked with Dr. Gutierrez about her job. When she went in, she was introduced to a new NP.

Dr. Gutierrez asked the ladies to join him in his office. He said, "Consuelo, meet Josephine. She is also the wife of a military man. She wants to work part-time. We have discussed you two splitting this job. You two can work out how to cover your patients. That way, when one of you must be away, the other can cover the job, and we will have uninterrupted service for all our patients."

Once he stopped speaking, Consuelo said, "Dr. Gutierrez, Josephine's husband and Jeff are in the same squadron. We have known each other four years. Josephine, I didn't know you were ready to go back to work? This is fantastic!"

The two women gave each other a hug. Dr. Gutierrez said, "Military people! I should have known you would know each other. I am now doubly happy. You two are already friends and are familiar with each other's personality. This should work out very well for the clinic."

Consuelo asked, "Josephine, how is your baby? Well, he really isn't an infant any longer, but he is still little. How old is he? Two?"

"Can you believe? Marshall will be three this fall. I have been happy to be home with him this long."

The conversations continued but were soon interrupted by Dr. Gutierrez. "Okay, ladies, old home week is over. Time to get to work."

A nurse said, "Consuelo, you have a patient in number five. Josephine, a lady is waiting for you in number eight."

Chapter 27

A year had passed since the death of Consuelo's father. Jeff had not been on any long missions, just a few days at a time. The family had settled into a comfortable routine. Deborah was in first grade and Peter in third grade.

Military people seem to know that when there is a lull in activity, it is just a matter of time until a disruption in daily activities will happen. Jeff came home one evening saying, "I have received orders for a transfer to another section here on base. We do not have to move! Let go celebrate tonight! Get a babysitter."

Excitedly Consuelo said, "Wait, wait one minute! What? A reassignment to another section here on base? What does this mean? Tell me quick! Does that mean you do not have to travel?"

"Whoa! Wait a minute. Girl, stop and take a deep breath!" He was laughing at her. "I will have to travel some. I will continue to fly some, but not long missions unless something ugly breaks out someplace in the world. Otherwise, you will have to put up with me right here at home! I am assigned to a Cultural and International Affairs section. Different cultural issues arise from time to time and a mediator is needed. I will be going through mediation training to earn the certification to perform these duties. They said, 'Who is better to represent cultural and international affairs that a Navajo Indian?' Anyway, my degree was in Political and Foreign Affairs. The air force feels they want me on this path. They want me to design a program that will supply a service to the particular needs of our diverse population." Then in a muffled tone of voice, he added, "They even mentioned, perhaps, sometime in the future, possibly an assignment as an air attaché."

"How exciting!" By now, Consuelo was dancing up and around the room, holding her hands above her head pretending that she was playing castanets.

Jeff was clapping his hands to a Latin beat, laughing. "Stop it! You are making me dizzy! Oh yes, that reminds me. I forgot to tell you the squadron is having a party. They were asking for dancers to volunteer for the entertainment. I volunteered you to do the flamenco and hat dance. But I made the stipulation that I would be the male dancer accompanying you. Guess we will need to practice. It has been a long time since we danced."

She stopped dancing and stared at him. "You what? But I haven't danced like that in years! Practice? You can rest assured we need a lot of practice! Otherwise, the crowd will think two crazy people dressed in Mexican costumes are out there doing a retro-combination of funky chicken/bunny hop!" By now they were both laughing until tears were dropping off their chins. He caught her in his arms and held her tightly and gave her a long kiss.

Peter and Deborah came running in to see what all the ruckus was about. They arrived just in time to see them kissing. In unison both kids said, "Eweeeeuuu! Not again!"

"How about going out to eat tomorrow night? It is a little late for tonight. How about a hotdog?"

As soon as the hastily put together meal was consumed, Consuelo opened a special box, carefully unwrapping castanets while Jeff opened a music app on his phone and began playing Mexican music. The parents began dancing. Peter and Deborah were clapping and cheering as their parents danced around the living room. Then the two children started imitating their parents. Jeff stopped to help Peter, and Consuelo began showing Deborah the correct posture and how to position her hands when she was playing castanets. She also showed her how to do the dance steps. The family was having so much fun that no one noticed that it was well past bedtime for the little ones. Baths and story time were hurried to keep the hour from getting any later before they went to bed.

The next morning, Deborah was tired and grumpy. She and Peter got into a big fuss. Eventually, a parent got involved in the squabble. Then the other parent got into it with that parent. Soon everyone appeared to have a black cloud over their heads as they walked out the door for school and work. Consuelo turned to Jeff for a kiss, and he was stiff as a board as he gave her a peck. She told him, "I'm sorry, Jeff."

He mumbled something and got in to his pickup and sped off.

Consuelo loaded the two kids into the SUV. Peter had his elbow on the armrest scowling out the window on his side of the car while Deborah mirrored his example on the opposite side of the car.

"Deborah, I know you are tired. I am sorry about that. Please apologize to Peter. He is your best friend. Tell him you are sorry you were unkind to him."

In a loud, unrepentant voice, with a scowl on her face, Deborah said, "But I am not sorry. He got to the bathroom before I did. He wouldn't get out when I told him to! I had to go!" By now, they were at school. As soon as the car came to a full stop, Deborah bolted out of the car in a full run. No usual goodbye or anything. Consuelo said, "Little buddy, have a good day. I am sorry she was such a pill today. Maybe she will be in a good mood after school."

Peter said, "Bye, Mom. I feel sorry for her teacher. I'll bet Deborah gets her name written on the board before noon."

It was Consuelo's day at the doctor's office. When she entered the door, the receptionist said, "Was it a rough morning, Consuelo?" "Yes, it was very rough. I need a minute before I meet my first patient. Deborah was on a tear this morning, and we all got into it. Ugh! It has been a long time since we have had a day to begin like this one. Do we have a full moon? As crazy as things are this morning, I truly think it must be."

The receptionists were laughing as Consuelo disappeared behind the ladies' room door. Consuelo looked in the mirror. Her hair was only half-combed, and she wasn't wearing makeup. Quickly she rectified the problem. She soon began her day. Her first patient was a grumpy old man. He agreed with nothing she had prescribed. He complained about the scales weighing too heavy, the electrodes on the EKG machine being too cold. The step was too high to get onto the examining table. The lights were too bright, and it was cold in the room. He was in an argumentative frame of mind. Consuelo asked if he would like the doctor to visit with him.

She was in the room with doctor and patient. Then the patient lambasted the doctor for no reason at all. Readings from examinations were presented to him. Some areas were elevated, but there were no imminent areas of major concerns. However, there were areas where he needed to exercise caution.

Dr. Gutierrez said, "George, how have things been at home since we saw you last? Any changes?" George was silent. Dr. Gutierrez continued, "We want to see you back in here in six weeks. If anything, unusual comes up, call us at once."

"I'll do that, Doctor. My wife has been out of town helping her sister for three weeks, and things have not been going well for me at home. I guess I better be honest with you. I have not been taking my medications as I should. She always sets my pills out for me."

Consuelo said, "Did you bring your medications with you today?" George said, "Yes!" He snapped, "I showed them to the nurse." George fumbled around in his jacket pocket and pulled out several bottles of medication.

"Dr. Gutierrez, I will get a daily medication dispenser and fill it for George to have ready for him each day. George, if you will wait in the waiting room, I will run to the drugstore and get a pill dispenser, and I will arrange your medications for you. If you will come back in the office as needed, we will fill the dispenser for you until your wife returns from caring for her sister."

While she was on an errand of mercy, she texted Jeff: "I am sorry things got so crazy and out of whack this morning. I am sorry. I love you."

She made her purchase and dashed back to the office. When she arrived the receptionist said, "There is something on your desk you might want to check out." She walked into her office, and there was a beautiful bouquet of red roses with a card attached. The note said, "Sorry that we all got off on a wrong foot this morning. Let's go out to dinner tonight. Can you get a babysitter?"

When Consuelo went to pick up the children after school, Deborah was moping along, not in a big hurry like usual. Peter got to the car first. He said, "I hope she has settled down. I don't like it when things are crazy like this morning. I am sorry, Mother."

Deborah crawled into the car, not giving a greeting of any kind. She buckled her seat belt folded her arms across her chest and sat quietly. Consuelo thought, *What do I do? Will I stir up a hornet's nest?* In her cheeriest voice, she said, "Hi, Deborah. How was your day?"

Deborah grunted.

After a long, awkward pause, Peter said, "Mother, today we played baseball, and I hit the ball a really long way! I got to second base!"

"I wish I could have seen that! That must have been very exciting." Deborah began to cry. Consuelo asked, "What's wrong, Deborah?" "I got my name on the board twice because I was grumpy and didn't do what the teacher said to do."

"I am sorry that you didn't get enough rest last night. Tonight, we will see to it that you get to bed on time. But what did you learn by getting your name on the board?"

"I will go to bed on time tonight, and I promise I will not be grumpy at everyone in the morning. I don't like the way it made me feel this morning. I was sad all day." She burst into tears. "I learned that if you do what teacher says to do, you will not get your name on the board." More tears flowed. "I didn't like getting my name on the board!"

Peter reached over and patted her on the shoulder and said, "It is okay, Deborah. We are all grumpy sometimes."

Wailing loudly, Deborah said, "But I got my name on the board, twice!"

"Tomorrow is a new day, and you will be nice and do what the teacher says to do. Then you will not get your name on the board ever again," said her much older and more mature brother.

Consuelo listened to them resolve the issue. Batting back tears, yet she had to smile. She thought, it is easy to be filled with wisdom and compassion and give sage advice when you are not the one who got in trouble.

Consuelo said, "Tonight Jacqueline will be babysitting while your daddy and I go out to dinner. You will have chicken nuggets for dinner. And yes, you will get to bed on time!"

Both kids said, "Yeah! Jacqueline!"

Deborah said, "We like Jacqueline. She is our favorite. She is fun."

Chapter 28

As a beautiful dinner was ending, Jeff said, "It looks like I will have to be gone again before my new job begins. I should be gone two or three weeks. I was hoping I wouldn't have to go back again anytime soon. It is hard on all of us when these missions come up."

Consuelo swallowed hard and battled back tears. "When do you leave?"

"They are thinking we will leave sometime next week. I hope it will not be for as long as they anticipate. I really like being home and hate to be away from you even when a pint-sized grumpy little person gets us all riled up."

"I promised her we will not do anything to prevent her from getting to bed on time tonight. Jacqueline has instructions to have them fed, bathed, and in bed by seven-thirty. She was tired and grumpy at school and would not do what the teacher told her to do, so she got her name on the board twice. That just broke her heart. I felt so sorry for her and felt guilty for us keeping her up past her bedtime. We know how she gets when she is tired. We were all having so much fun last night; the time just got away from me. Oh! Will you be leaving before the squadron party?"

"Yes, I will be leaving before the party. You will be dancing with Major Jose Ramirez. Consuelo, I am tempted to go AWOL! The thought of you dancing with that good-looking guy really gets me right here!" And with a clenched fist, he thumped on his chest and dramatically signaled to his heart, acting wounded.

"Sweetie, he can't hold a candle to you. You are the best-looking guy in the squadron—and the best dancer too. I will sacrifice and dance with Major Jose Ramirez," she said jokingly. "You know the old saying about a substitute being a poor excuse for the real thing. There is no substitute for my Navajo Eagle, a.k.a., Jeff." She gave him a teasing look and burst out laughing.

He just shook his head. "What can I say to that?" Both laughed merrily.

The week sped by. Jeff was now hugging his family goodbye, saying, "I hope to see you in a couple of weeks." As in all the times in the past when he left for a mission, the loneliness was overpowering when he walked out the door.

Deborah said, "I don't like it when Daddy has to leave us to go fly his airplane." Consuelo attempted to console her. She said, "I know, sweetie. It hurts my heart too. We just must stay very busy and make the days go by quickly. Then, pretty soon, we can prepare for him to come home."

Peter said, "Can we have a special dinner and a party when he comes home? You two can dance, and maybe Deborah and I will also."

Deborah said, "Yes, then I will go to bed early so I won't be grumpy."

"Okay, grab your things and let's get you to school."

"Do you go to work today, or is this Mrs. Josephine's day?" Peter asked.

"This is Mrs. Josephine's day. I have some errands to run and things to do. I will stay busy and make the day go by fast, so I can come pick you up at school."

Peter said, "I have a ballgame after school. Can you come watch me play?" Deborah clapped her hands. "Yeah, I want to go. Can we go see him play ball?"

"Sure. We will be there. Do you have everything for the game? Bye, guys. I'll see you later. Love you."

"Love you," they both said as they dashed out of the car and joined their friends, who were waiting for them. Just as she drove away from the school zone, her cell phone rang. It was Dr. Gutierrez's office.

"Josephine has been in a car accident on her way to work. Can you cover for her? She is banged up some with scrapes and bruises. The other car took the main brunt of the impact. Josephine is okay. No serious injuries. She is just very shaken."

Consuelo said that she would be a little late and explained that she planned to attend her son's ballgame after school. The caller said, "We understand. Come cover for Josephine. Get here as soon as you can."

Her mind was whirling, attempting to make all the necessary changes that were on her calendar. She was to try on her costume for the squadron dance, try on shoes, practice dancing with Major Ramirez, and run several other errands. Where to start first?

And so, the first day Jeff was away had begun. Funny, she thought. I always measure time by the number of days into Jeff's missions until something goes wrong. Thank goodness for hands-free phone service. She called the squadron building and asked for Major Ramirez. Soon he picked up the phone. She explained about Josephine being in a car accident and that she was covering for her at the doctor's office. They arranged another time to practice. Next, she called the dress shop and changed the appointment for a fitting of her dress.

Once at the office, she quickly reviewed the schedule of patients for the day. It appeared to be a relatively light day. But never trust a 'relatively light day' will stay that way, she thought.

There were two or three walk-ins with significant problems that required more time than normal. Soon she was behind for the day. She worked straight through lunch as she attempted to catch up. The 'light day' turned into a frantic rat race.

Late in the afternoon, Dr. Gutierrez walked into to her office. "I am not scheduled for anyone the rest of the afternoon. Go on to your son's ballgame. Thank you for coming in on such short notice. I really appreciate your flexibility. We would have been in a mess without you. We can handle it from here on. Tomorrow your full-time schedule will begin. I'll see you then until Josephine recovers from her automobile accident.

Consuelo and Deborah were seated behind home plate. Peter was looking for them. His face lit up with a big smile when he saw them. He hit the ball, and it landed between first and second base. He made it safely to first base. He turned and looked back at his mom and gave a thumb-up signal. She and Deborah were clapping wildly.

Unfortunately, his team lost. But Consuelo told him, "You really played well. I am so proud of you for doing your very best. Let's go get a Chunky Monkey."

The first week was soon history. Jeff called when he could. His schedule halfway around the world did not always fit with her schedule, making it difficult to have phone calls. In all the hectic schedule, Major Ramirez and Consuelo did work in a few practices. Peter and Deborah sat and watched several times, but most of the times they stayed with friends until she could pick them up. When Jeff would call, he was always curious how the practice sessions were going and expressed how sorry he was not be there with her.

'The night of the squadron party arrived. Jacqueline was the babysitter of choice. The kids oooed and aahhed over Consuelo's beautiful dress and the adornments that decorated her beautiful black hair. Her makeup was applied to perfection. Jacqueline took her picture with Consuelo's phone and sent it to Jeff. Consuelo was standing, with chin up in a classic flamenco dance position. She had one hand held gracefully over her head, the other hand was holding onto her brilliant red skirt as it flared out in yards of brilliant color.

Electricity was in the air with excitement and anticipation as men dressed handsomely in mess-dress uniforms and women in lovely party dresses walked up the red carpet leading to the entrance of the building. Interspersed in the parade were the dancers dressed in colorful costumes from their home of origin or their heritage. A cameraman was positioned to capture each couple as they made their entrance. Major Ramirez met Consuelo and escorted her up the carpeted walkway into the area where they were to wait until their time to perform. When he saw her, he said, "Wow! You are beautiful. Jeff doesn't know what he is missing out on. But he will know. The guys in Guam will be watching this show. It is being live-streamed to them, so let's make this really

This Last Mission

good. Let's show the crowd what traditional Mexican dancing is like. If Jeff is flying, it will be recorded for him to see when he returns to base. The evening began with a full program. Dancers were from Japan, Vietnam, Germany, and several other countries. There were singers as well. One was an Irish tenor. One guy from Germany yodeled. A Scotsman played the bagpipe. It was an amazing evening. Major Ramirez's and Consuelo's dances were flawless. During the program, both noticed the Squadron Commander and Base Commander as they left the area. They looked at each other and Consuelo said, "I wonder what that was all about?"

The entertainment for the evening continued. Eventually, the last song was sung, and last dance was performed. Just as the curtain was falling behind the performers after the grand finale, the base commander appeared on the stage. Someone came to Consuelo and escorted her and Major Ramirez to a room at the back of the stage. They had some information to give her in private. Her heart was filled with joy. With happy anticipation she thought, was Jeff back? Or is he on the phone?

After Consuelo and Major Ramirez had left the stage, the base commander took the microphone and said, "Ladies and gentlemen. I have an announcement to make. We have lost a B-2. I do not want you leaving this event tonight and seeing this information splashed on all the TV screens in town, including on your own home set. The B-2 was one of our own. An airliner was in the vicinity of the crash, and a passenger recorded the last moments of smoke trailing the plane followed by an explosion. That video is now on TV screens across the nation. The pilots ejected but have not been recovered. A search-and-rescue is underway. We have pinpoint accuracy as to where they were. The families are being notified right now."

Someone called out, "Who is it?" Then there were hushed, muffled voices. Some were crying. So many questions. Information like this sends shockwaves through a military community. Only this time they had names. But they did not have information as to whether it was to be a rescue or a recovery.

The commander said, "The pilots are Major Atsa (Jeff) Blackhawk and Major Charlie Swaine. We currently have people with both of their wives. Others have called their parents. Pray for our pilots and their families. Goodnight, ladies and gentlemen. I am saddened to end such a lovely evening with a message like this. Be safe driving home. Be sure to pray for the pilots and their families."

Chapter 29

The US military called on allies who had ships in the area where the big plane had gone down to assist in the search and rescue. Several US Navy vessels sailed toward the area at top speed. Air force planes were sent to fly over the area looking for signs of the two airmen floating in the water. Television stations were saying that the plane had exploded and had gone down in a ball of flames over international waters. No signals were received from the two downed pilots.

A local television station said, "The B-2 bomber went down in the Gulf of Alaska, just off the Aleutian Islands. The water is frigid, and life cannot be sustained for any length of time. Hope is fading for the two downed airmen."

Once back home, when Consuelo heard this information on television, she fell to her knees, weeping and praying, asking God for mercy and safety for the two downed pilots. Several squadron wives were with Consuelo and others with Margaret. Each wife had a cluster of friends who stayed with her and cared for the children and prepared meals.

Pastor Johnson and his wife, Ruby, were with Consuelo and the children when she attempted to explain that their father's airplane had a problem and had gone down but that he had ejected from the plane before it went down. Sobbing, Peter said, "But, Mama, we heard a lady on television say that Daddy's plane blew up in a big fireball." Deborah was wailing angrily. "I want my daddy to come home right now!" Wiping tears, Consuelo, said, "I know, Deborah. I do too."

Later that evening, Consuelo and the children had their usual Bible story and prayer time. Deborah prayed, "Please, dear God, please don't let our daddy be dead."

The next days were days of silence from the air force. They said they had no new information, but the search was still in progress. They were not giving up.

Josephine filled in for Consuelo at the office. The children missed two days of school before a counselor told Consuelo that the children needed to be back in a familiar daily routine.

Reluctantly, Consuelo took them back to school. Likewise, she was told to resume her duties at the doctor's office. She needed to maintain a regular schedule.

She was in daily contact with her family and Jeff's family. She told them, "As soon as I hear from him, and I feel that I will, I will contact you at once. Please keep praying for him. I can't give up! Pray for all of us."

In the following days, weeks, and months, life went on for the little family: church activities on Sundays, the usual childhood sniffles and scrapes, daily chores, and homework. Abuela came to stay with the little family and help Consuelo for two weeks during the difficult time. The children were happy to have their grandmother visit them. Consuelo watched the interaction of grandparent and grandchildren and thought, there is such a strong bond between them.

Deborah got braces. Peter broke an arm playing ball with neighborhood boys. Abuela was a great help and comfort for him as he got used to doing things with one arm. The children had night-terrors involving airplanes crashing or exploding. Both children would awaken screaming in terror from the realistic dreams. Both children experienced a plummet in grades at school. The school counselor saw them frequently, letting them talk about their scary dreams and how sad they were that their daddy's airplane had crashed.

There was the usual maintenance of the SUV. The lawn had to be mowed. Consuelo struggled to care for her little family and maintain her job and the home, doing the chores Jeff normally took care of when he was home. Abuela's visit could not have come at a better time.

Consuelo thought, *Oh, Jeff, I wish you were here to do this. I miss you. Jeff, if you are alive, where are you? Jeff, this cannot be happening to us. Oh, get a grip Consuelo! He will come home.* Please, *God, hear my prayers. Dear God, I can't give up. Give me strength, merciful Father. Please find Jeff and bring him home. Help me, Lord. Help all of us including Margaret and her children.*

She called Margaret to check on her and the children. The two wives spent a lot of time together, each trying to encourage and help the other as best she could. They ate frequent meals together and even spent many nights with one another to push away the darkest loneliness. It was easier to do that at Margaret's house because her baby was still sleeping in a crib. Consuelo and her children would bring sleeping bags and air mattresses. It was being together that was important. The other woman knew the pain and suffering the other was experiencing and knew how to pull her out of the deep pit of grief or to be there to lend support.

The children were together so much they called each other our air force cousins, and they turned these times into a spend-the-night party.

Chapter 30

Weeks later, the Pacific Command located in Honolulu, Hawaii, along with other military bases around the Pacific basin were searching night and day for traces of the aircraft and two downed airmen.

Three weeks had passed since Abuela had gone home. Colonel Harrison and Gerry came to Consuelo's home to check on her and the children. They had been with Margaret, Charlie Swaine's wife. They had been in phone contact, but this time they wanted to add the personal touch. He said, "Consuelo, we are still searching, but it is not looking hopeful. Some time back the search was changed from rescue to recovery. I am sure you had figured that out by now. I am sorry to be the one to tell you. Also, I hate to suggest this, but a couple of men from our squadron will bring Jeff's pickup and personal effects home."

Consuelo said with strong emphasis, "Okay. Bring it all home tomorrow! I am not scheduled to work, so I will be here. But, sir, I am not giving up. I believe in miracles. I believe Jeff will show up on my doorstep one day. All I have left is hope and my faith in God. I must hold on and be strong for my children. Thank you, and you, Gerry, for your support. But I am not ready to give up hope. I can't give up! I cannot accept the fact that Jeff might be...I cannot accept the obvious." Hot, silent tears flowed down her cheeks.

With tenderness and compassion, Colonel Harrison asked, "What can we do for you? Can we take you and the children to dinner?"

With a heavy sigh, she said, "Thank you, sir. I do not know what to do next. I am simply at a loss as to my next step. I have never felt so helpless. My mind is in a muddle. The only thing I can do is just stay put and hold on until I can figure it out. Thank you for listening to me ramble on. Yes, sir, dinner would be nice. I have not been eating very well, even though Margaret and I do try to get together often for a meal. Anyway, maybe getting out and having an adult conversation will help…. I just keep waiting for a phone call. Here I go rattling on again."

"Okay. That does it. Peter, Deborah, come here."

They both came running down the hallway. Peter said, "Yes, sir?"

"We are going out to eat. Do you want to go? After dinner we may even have a Chunky Monkey. I have heard how you like that ice cream." Both children in unison said, "Yes, sir!"

The following day, two men brought Jeff's pickup home. Consuelo met them in the driveway and asked them to park it in the garage.

After they left, she got in the pickup. One of Jeff's flight jackets was lying on the seat. She picked it up tenderly and clutched it to her breast. Then all the pent-up emotions of her loss and loneliness came pouring out. She wept until she was exhausted. She buried her face in the jacket and inhaled his scent. A second wave of grief overwhelmed her when she prayed, "Dear God, the unthinkable keeps trying to creep into my mind. Help me to stay strong and believe that one day I will see him again."

This was the first of many visits to the pickup Consuelo would make as she dealt with her grief and loss.

Three months had now passed, and the US Government had no information on what had happened to Jeff and Charlie. Their families were struggling. Each painful day of uncertainty and not knowing what had happened to Jeff and Charlie faded into the next day.

In the native village of Afognak, Alaska, the Tribal Council was holding a meeting. A shy fisherman, an Alutiiq, hesitantly asked to address the council. He said, "More than three months ago, we saw a fireball in the sky while my brothers and I were in our kayaks fishing. We saw a Russian trawler pick up two bundles from the water. They lifted the bundles carefully onto the ship and were making a lot of noise about it being humans. Do you think the men came from the fireball? My brothers have televisions and they say they heard that the fireball was an airplane. Is this important information? My brothers say we should report this to someone. But who do we tell?"

"How did you know what they were saying?" a councilman asked.

"We were close by the trawler and sound carries across the water. Also, we speak Russian and our own native language, as do most of the people in my village. We saw the ship. And we know what Russian trawlers look like. This was a medium- sized trawler."

The leader of the council said, "I will be going to Anchorage next week. I will report this information to the police. They will know what to do with your information. Thank you for sharing this with us."

Shortly after the crash, the US Navy had moved ships with sophisticated diving equipment into the area where the B-2 had gone down. They were searching for debris or any equipment that might give them a clue as to what happened to the big plane. However, winter's grip would soon take hold on the area. They were attempting to retrieve any debris before the possibility of early winter storms.

They remained late into the fall until ice began to form on the ships and equipment. Soon, there would be little they could do except wait until the spring thaw.

The military had voice recordings that had been transmitted the day of the crash. The pilots were discussing emergency procedures. They gave their location and the problems they were experiencing with the plane. They were descending to a lower level in the event they had to abandon the aircraft. That was the last transmission.

After the Russians pulled the two unconscious men out of the water, they immediately took them to the sick bay. They removed their flights suits, placed the men in warm, dry clothing, began warm IVs, and wrapped them in heated blankets. The medic in charge treated the men with compassion and remained with them, changing out warm blankets in an attempt to raise their body temperature. Someone was with the men around the clock.

They were monitored for pneumonia and other signs of exposure to the cold water. The captain said, "They were in the water about fifteen minutes or longer before we could reach them. Their flight suits were not insulated for frigid water."

The captain struggled with what to do with the men. He thought, they could be used for ransom. Who are they? Do I tell the government about these two? What do I do? They could be bargaining chips. He did not put a message out over the airwaves that he had rescued the two Americans. He was biding his time and studying his options.

In Anchorage, the council leader reported the information given to the council by an Alutiiq. In turn, the information was delivered to authorities at Elmendorf Air Force Base, who contacted the Pentagon and the Pacific Command.

By this time, an early winter cold front had arrived and had its grip firmly on the Aleutian Islands and all of Alaska. The man who had delivered the message lived in a small village in an outlying area many miles away. The councilmen were not sure how to contact him. He just appeared in their meeting and had disappeared as quietly as he had come. All they knew was he and his brothers were fishermen. One of the councilmen thought he might know the name of a cousin of the man.

By the time the US military heard the message provided by a councilman about a Russian trawler picking up the two flyers, the ship had long since moved on. The councilman could not identify the name of the man who had told him about seeing the Americans plucked out of the ocean. The military was frustrated with the limited information they had received and thought it might be someone seeking attention during a high-profile story. When America inquired of the Russians about the two flyers, they denied knowing anything about the two airmen.

Chapter 31

More than four months had passed since the Russian trawler had plucked Jeff and Charlie out of the frigid waters of the Gulf of Alaska, after the crew saw a giant fireball and horrendous explosion. They also witnessed two parachutes drifting down and splashing into the ocean. The captain of the trawler ordered the ship to go in the direction of the two airmen. The airmen were suffering from serious hypothermia when they were rescued. They were whisked into the medical bay and treatment was begun.

Within days, both men were fully recovered.

The trawler crept across the choppy, frigid waters, farther out into international waters around the Aleutian Islands and up into the Bering Sea, attempting to return to port.

They had been on a fishing trip, and the freezer space on the ship was filled to capacity. This was their last fishing trip for the season, and they had stayed beyond the time to return to port because of the bountiful catch. The danger of staying past the last day of fishing was encountering an early winter storm. This was evidently the case, as the farther north they traveled, the more ice they encountered. Going was very slow because one of the engines was experiencing problems. The captain was afraid that it would break down and they would become stranded. Eventually, one engine quit in open waters. The ship limped along at half power as it encountered heavy North Sea waves. There were no nearby ports where they could take shelter until the storm had passed. Tension was high aboard the ship. Being stranded near the Bering Sea was a very serious matter.

Theda Yager

Two days or more were wasted as they labored to repair the engine. Eventually the engine was repaired, and the journey continued, but they had lost valuable time.

After they had passed through the Bering Strait, they became trapped in ice. The ship was coated in ice from giant waves that had splashed over the craft while they were in open water. Now, they were entrapped in a sea of ice. They could move neither forward or backward.

They were in international waters and sent out a message calling for help. Fortunately, a privately-owned icebreaker, the Denali IV, had been in a harbor in the Aleutian Islands for repairs and had only recently resumed their journey to the Arctic. The icebreaker was flying an American flag. They answered the call for help by the stricken vessel. They rescued the trawler and opened a channel for the trawler to continue their journey into Russian waters, where a Russian icebreaker would help them if they ran into more trouble.

The captain of the Denali IV spoke through an interpreter and said, "You are out pretty late for fishing." The trawler captain replied, "Yes, we are. We pushed the timeline and got caught out too late in the season to make it back to port. Our catch was outstanding. Then we had trouble with one of the engines on our ship. And, sir, I think I pulled something out of the water you will be very interested in. Since you have come to rescue us, I am giving you the two bundles we pulled out of the water—two airmen. Their airplane crashed several months ago, maybe five months ago now. We plucked them out of frigid waters. They were suffering from hypothermia when we retrieved them. I must tell you, one of the men speaks a language we have never heard. The name on his dog tag is Atsa Blackhawk. He looks like island people, only taller. He is not from any of the tribes in this area. I have relatives living in the Aleutian Islands. I know languages of many tribes, but not his language. We call him the 'quiet one.' These men have worked on our ship. They are very knowledgeable. The 'quiet one' repaired one of our engines that had broken down. Can we transfer them over to you? Or do we contact someone else?"

Captain Walters said, "We are going into an Alaskan port, and we will turn them over to the authorities."

Chapter 32

Word spread rapidly across the military network reporting that Jeff and Charlie had been located on a Russian trawler. They reported that the Russian trawler had been marooned in ice when they were rescued by a commercial icebreaker. The captain of the rescued vessel turned the two airmen over to them. The US military called the Russian captain a "hero" for rescuing the men.

Colonel Harrison and Gerry called Consuelo and Margaret Swaine to meet them at their home. There was something they wanted to discuss. Both wives hastily arranged for babysitters and drove to the Colonel's home. When they entered the home, Gerry said, "Ladies, have a seat. Can I get you something to drink?"

Puzzled, the two looked at each other. Margaret said, "What is this? What is going on?"

Colonel Harrison said, "Have a seat. There is something I want to tell you two. I want you to hear it from me before you hear it on the television or somewhere else. This information is to be released to the public very soon. We are attempting to inform you two and your parents before everyone hears it on their television sets. Your husbands have been found—alive. They are safe and well. A privately-owned icebreaker has them. They were rescued by a Russian trawler. Sometime later, the trawler became trapped in ice as it attempted to make its way to home port. A privately-owned icebreaker, the Denali IV, rescued the ice-trapped Russian vessel. That is when the trawler captain handed over

Theda Yager

Jeff and Charlie to them. Your husbands are safe. I do not know how soon they will be coming home. There are many details to take care of regarding transportation and so on. Right now, they are on a vessel in a sea of ice. The icebreaker must get to an area where an airplane can land safely and pick up Jeff and Charlie. The icebreaker is keeping a channel open in a frozen ocean for oil tankers and other seagoing vessels. Next stop is Point Barrow, Alaska. That is the northernmost point in the United States. When they reach that town, they will be picked up by the United States Air Force. But, like I said, a lot of details must be worked out. We will be keeping you up to date on each step of this experience."

Both wives were holding on to each other and began laughing and crying at the same time. Consuelo kept saying, "I just knew they would come home! I never gave up my faith in God that He would bring them home. Thank you, Jesus!"

Both women gave the colonel and Gerry hugs and thanked them for this wonderful news. Now they had to get home and share the news with their children.

Chapter 33

The crew gathered around the two airmen welcoming them aboard. Captain Walters of the Denali IV turned to Jeff and said, "So, you are the quiet one."

Jeff gave a half laugh and said, "Maybe, but that actually is a misnomer. When I regained conscientiousness in the sick bay with strange men standing over me, speaking in a language I could not understand, all I could think of was give them my name, rank, and serial number—only I gave it to them in my first language, Navajo. They were looking me over and changed their languages several times. I didn't know where Charlie was, or if he was alive or dead. All I could think of was survival, so I continued speaking in Navajo. Later, when I saw Charlie and he was okay, I signaled him to remain silent regarding my language. He said something about Russians."

Charlie spoke up. "They kept saying in Russian, 'the Silent One is an islander. But he doesn't speak any of the languages that we are familiar with.' They were very puzzled. They kept looking at his dog tag, Atsa Blackhawk. They kept saying, 'which tribe does he belong to?' I kept listening to them speak Russian but continued to speak in English through an interpreter. Oh, for your information, I speak Russian. My mother is Russian. I learned from her, and then in college I majored in linguistics. But don't ask me to interpret for the 'silent one.' That is a language I cannot figure out. By this time in our journey, we could not reveal our languages for fear of angering our rescuers, so we just played along. I am sure the silent one's head was about to blow off his shoulders from wanting to speak so often—this guy likes to talk better than anyone you have ever met! Someday this experience may be funny. But at the time, we were in a survival mode. We did not know what their intentions were. We kept waiting for the Russian military to board the trawler and apprehend us."

Jeff chimed in, "Charlie and I saw things that needed to be done on the ship, and we began to do our part. But I must say, that was only after we had recovered from being seasick. Those waves were higher than the trawler. We were both so seasick that I kept wondering if we would live or die. That was the roughest boat ride I had ever experienced—until now. How long does it take you to get used to the sound and feel of this ship bumping, scraping, ramming huge chunks of ice and the creaking and moaning of this vessel? How do you know if it is a bad sound or a good sound? An airplane pilot listens for any unusual sound. How do you know what an unusual sound is with everything going on around this ship?"

Charlie said, "After what we have been through the past several months, when I hit the bunk tonight, I will consider these unusual sounds to be a lullaby."

Consuelo dashed into the house and breathlessly called the children. "Jacqueline, will you stay with us a few more minutes, please? I have something to tell everyone."

Deborah and Peter were standing beside her. "What is it? Why are you so excited?"

She said, "They found your daddy and Charlie. They are alive and well. A Russian fishing boat had picked them up when they parachuted from their plane. Then, when the boat was going back to their home port, they became trapped in ice and could not go forward or backward. They were frozen in place. The captain of the fishing boat called for help. A private icebreaker, the Denali IV, came to rescue them. Then the Russian ship that had rescued your daddy was rescued by an American icebreaker. The Russian captain gave your daddy and Charlie to the

This Last Mission

commercial ice breaker's captain! Your daddy and Charlie have been rescued. They will be home sometime soon."

Deborah shouted, "I knew it! I asked God to please do not let my daddy be dead, and He didn't!" Dancing around the room in typical Deborah style, she said, "Yeah God! Thank you, thank you, for taking care of my daddy."

"Is Daddy going to call us? Is he getting on a C-130 and coming home like before?" Peter asked.

"I am not sure what kind of plane he will fly home in, and I do not know when. We will have to Google icebreakers and see what kind of ship your daddy is on. Also, we will have to read about what an icebreaker does. As I understand it, the Denali IV was out in the ocean breaking thick ice to make channels for ships or oil tankers, so they could get through to their ports. When the Denali IV arrives at a place called Point Barrow, Alaska, your daddy will get on an airplane and come home. It will not be right away. They are way out on the sea. We will have to look up all this information on the computer."

Jacqueline said, "I've got to see this! This is way too cool! I can't wait to get home and research this."

"Good point, Jacqueline. And I need to call our parents and our pastor. Thank you for staying with Peter and Deborah. They love it when you are here with them. Thank you."

Chapter 34

Charlie and Jeff spent a lot of time with Captain Walters on the bridge, observing how he searched out areas of open water or ice that was not thick. They found it fascinating to hear him talk about various trips they had made to the North Pole. He told them of rescue missions they had assisted with.

Charlie asked, "What about polar bear? How far do they roam from land?"

The captain replied, "They have been seen hundreds of miles from land. They could have drifted on ice floes until they could reach solid ice, and then they are also strong swimmers. When they are in open water, they search for seals. If ice is not too thick, they search for air holes where seals come up for a breath of air. The bears break through those places, and they catch and eat the seals. They are not afraid of humans. They are very dangerous animals. It is amazing to see a solitary bear, usually a male, or perhaps a female with cubs, out on a frozen sea of ice. It doesn't happen often, but it is possible to spot one on rare occasions. A solitary animal will stand at a distance and watch our ship as it goes along. I would like to know what they are thinking when they see our ship going through the ice and pushing it aside."

The next day at school, Peter and Deborah told teachers and fellow students about their daddy being rescued by a Russian fishing vessel and then how a commercial icebreaker had rescued the Russians. Teachers pulled up pictures of the commercial icebreaker on computers for the children to see.

Consuelo was telling the same story at the doctor's office. Everyone was celebrating that the two men had been found alive and well.

While Consuelo was sharing her exciting news, Josephine called the office and said, "Put me on speaker phone, I want everyone to hear what I have to say. I am at the hospital with my son, Marshall. He was admitted late last week. It is a good thing I worked only Tuesday and Thursday last week. Marshall was hospitalized Thursday night. The doctors are not sure what's wrong with him. He has been sick, off and on, all of his life. They are running tests and say that he will be transferred to a specialty children's hospital in Minneapolis that deals with rare and unusual illnesses. I am sorry, but I do not know when I will be back to work. It depends on how my little guy does. They are flying us out later today. My husband is in Guam, so things are a little complicated. Marshall's doctors have put us in touch with a genetic and rare diseases center. Say a prayer for him and for us. I will call you when I can. Oh yes, one more thing. I had planned to tell you next week. I am almost three months pregnant. The doctors are now concerned about our unborn baby if Marshall's illness is genetic. In that case, it is possible that our new baby may be affected, Pray really hard for all of us."

Dr. Gutierrez said, "Consuelo will cover for you just as you have for her. You two have been a good team. Take care of little Marshall. Let us know what they find out. We will all pray for you. We pray that it is a lookalike disease, or something that is treatable and not one of the rare genetic cases."

After Josephine hung up, Dr. Gutierrez shook his head and said, "How do you military wives do it?"

Consuelo replied, "Doctor of all people, you know that you do what you have to do. You just prioritize. In the medical field, when there are multiple serious cases, we do triage. Well, that is sort of what we have to do as military dependents."

"Now, please continue telling us about your good news. Your husband and the other gentleman have been found alive? Please, tell us how this came about and when will they be coming home?"

After Consuelo had given a shortened synopsis of what happened, she concluded, "That is all I know at this time. And I see the waiting room is filling up. Don't you think we ought to get to work around here?"

Dr. Gutierrez replied, "Yes, but it is important that we as a team understand what our teammates are experiencing in their lives. Thank you for sharing. Now to work, everyone!"

The day had begun. It was a full day and two of Consuelo's favorite patients had appointments. They were Mrs. Berkley and Mr. Jones. When she saw their names on the list she smiled. Today she could use a friendly visit and encouraging smile from these two people. Mr. Jones was first. Consuelo reviewed his chart before entering the examining room. When she went in the room she said," I see you have lost twenty pounds since I saw you last. Congratulations! I am so proud of you. Hmm, now, I'll bet that good-looking widow lady has taken notice of you!"

He ducked his head and grinned like a bashful schoolboy. He replied, "'Yes, we have been on a couple of dates. Say, did I hear on the TV that a B-2 went down? That was your husband's plane? I recognized the name Blackhawk. I prayed for you and your family. Didn't they say he and his co-pilot have been found alive? Consuelo, I am so sorry for what you have been through, but it sounds like there will be a happy ending this time. I came in today to visit with you, not that I had any medical reasons. I do not need a new prescription. I do not have any issues. Just mark this down as a social call, if that insurance form has such a thing on it. You have been important to me in the past. I want to be here for you and your family."

"Thank you, sir. You are correct. He has been rescued and will be coming home sometime soon. We do not know just when. Thank you for your concern and good thoughts and prayers. Now, since you are here, let me check your blood pressure and listen to your heart. We don't want anything sneaking up on us."

She asked the usual questions regarding his medication, diet, and exercise program. "Hmm, your blood pressure is significantly elevated. We need to do something about that. Are you taking your meds as prescribed? I want to take it again, and I want to listen to your chest again. Then I want Dr. Gutierrez to pop in and see you. He may want to get you on a different medication. Let's see. When did you have an EKG? Looks like you are due to have one. The nurse will get you set up. I will be right back."

Dr. Gutierrez was in the hallway reviewing a chart before entering a treatment room when Consuelo approached him and said, "Can I have a minute of your time? I am concerned about Mr. Jones. I am hearing something I have not heard before when I listen to his chest, and his blood pressure is significantly elevated. He is being set up for an EKG. Would you take a look at him, please?"

Suddenly the routine visit turned into a different experience. Dr. Gutierrez entered the examining room with Consuelo, and the two of them looked at the printout from the EKG machine.

The doctor spoke. "Let me listen to your chest. Mr. Jones, I am so happy you came in today. This routine visit is not routine. I must hospitalize you. We need to do some tests we cannot do here. You are fortunate to be in our office at this time. Since you live alone, I am transporting you to the heart hospital via ambulance. Consuelo spotted something going on with your old ticker, and we want to check it out."

Consuelo asked, "Is there anyone you want us to call? Maybe the widow down the street? Your pastor or priest?"

"I have a dog, a big chocolate lab. Maybe the widow lady, Mrs. Culpepper, will care for him until I can get back home. I will give you her number."

The day was a busy one. One patient after another. Last appointment of the day was Mrs. Berkley. When she entered the door, she was walking with a walker. Consuelo went to meet her and held the door for her. "Mrs. Berkley, what happened?" she began.

In a saucy tone of voice, as in olden days, she responded, "Sometimes you just ask too many questions!" Then she looked at Consuelo and laughed. Then added, "Well, you do!"

"Okay, so I do. So, what happened to you? Have you been skateboarding?"

"I entered a half-marathon for old geezers my age. I was almost to the finish line—leading the pack, I might add—when I stepped into a hole in the pavement and fell. I tore up my knee. They did surgery, and it is healing slowly. But it is healing. I plan to enter again next year.

"But, dearie, I heard about your husband's airplane going down. I sat down and bawled my heart out. It reminded me of when I lost my dear husband in the Vietnam War. Did they ever find those two men?"

Consuelo reached out to the older woman and caught her hands and told her about the good news of them being located on an icebreaker. They had been rescued by a Russian fishing trawler and handed over to a commercial icebreaker somewhere up above the Bering Strait.

Mrs. Berkley pulled Consuelo to her and gave her a big hug. She said "Oh, honey, I am so happy for you. It sounds like you will have a happy ending."

More than two weeks had passed when Josephine contacted the office. She said, "A diagnosis has been determined. Marshall has sickle cell anemia. Our new baby may or may not have it. The baby will be tested when it is born. So, only time will tell. They were surprised that it wasn't diagnosed before now since he has been a sickly little boy. He began having trouble close to his first birthday. And he has always been small for his age; plus, he has low energy. Four or five generations back, my husband and I both had black ancestors, and apparently the sickle cell gene was passed down through both of our lineages. This was discovered through genetic testing. Apparently, we are both carriers. Maybe that is why it was not discovered earlier. Anyway, we will be home in a few days. He will have times when he will do well, then other times where he is not doing well at all and will need to be hospitalized. I will call when I am back home."

This Last Mission

Consuelo called Jolene to see if she had moved and how things were going for her. The divorce was final. The home was part of her settlement; also, since they had been married more than twenty years, half of her husband's retirement pay would be hers. She had sold the home and now had purchased a small townhouse in Richmond, Virginia, near her family. She was working and was beginning to get on her feet financially. She said, "I feel I am regaining my psychological health. There are times when I have my moments, but otherwise, I am doing well."

She asked about Consuelo, Jeff, and the children. Consuelo explained that Jeff and Charlie were fine, but their plane had crashed. Both men had been ejected and were later rescued. They would be home in a few weeks.

The two friends had a pleasant conversation and promised to keep in touch.

Chapter 35

It had been several days since Margaret and Consuelo had been together. They agreed to meet at a child-friendly place for a meal and to visit while the children played on the indoor play equipment.

Margaret said, "I am so tired of trying to pretend that I am strong. I'm not. I am just falling apart on the inside. Consuelo, can we hold it together until our guys get home? I can only be honest with you because you understand. It is a day-to-day struggle."

Consuelo responded, "Yes, it is. But Margaret, we have to do it. We can't give in to our feelings. I just want to curl up in a ball and bawl my eyes out, but my head knows I can't do that. Instead I go to the garage and get in Jeff's pickup and cry my heart out. I feel close to him when I am in there. Then, there are my children and you and your children to think about. Our guys are in their struggle, and so are we. They are trying to get home to us. We must keep things going until they walk through that door and give us a hand with stuff. If I never mow another lawn, it will be too soon!"

Margaret laughed. "I know what you mean. I am not a gardener. Charlie loves to work in the yard. He will probably say, 'What have you done to my yard?' It's not what I did to it. It is what I haven't done to it. I better go to Home Depot and buy out the garden center and plant flowers all over the yard before he gets home." Both women burst into laughter at that ridiculous thought.

Both women were laughing about their lack of green thumbs when the children came back to the table. Deborah said, "Mommy, I don't feel good." Consuelo put her hand on the child's flushed forehead. "You have a fever! Oh Margaret, what have we exposed you to? We better go home." Margaret said, "I will call you tomorrow to see how Deborah is doing." They all said goodnight and went their separate ways.

Consuelo asked Deborah several questions, and the child said, "My arms and legs hurt, and my head hurts really bad! My throat hurts. Oh, Mommy, I am going to throw up."

And she did, in the car.

Peter was gagging. He said, "Deborah, stop it. You are making me sick too. Momma, I am going to throw up." Fortunately, Consuelo had pulled the car off the side of the road and Peter opened the door. At least it didn't mess up his side of the car! Fortunately, Consuelo carried a roll of paper towels in the car. She cleaned up the mess as best she could.

After several stops, the little family arrived at home. Consuelo took Deborah's temperature: 103 degrees. She called the pediatrician and was told to take her to the ER at children's hospital.

Consuelo grabbed a small trash can to put in the back seat with Deborah, an air freshener, plastic bags, and more paper towels. Soon they pulled into the children's hospital's parking lot. She struggled to get a very sick child into the hospital for her to be checked out.

By now, Deborah was shivering and shaking with chills and fever. A nurse hurried them into an examining room. Soon a doctor came to attend the sick child.

The doctor said, "We are seeing a lot of strep throat. Let's check you out and see if this is what is making you feel so bad. Okay Deborah, let me look in your ears. Hmmm, do I see a purple bunny rabbit in there? Yes! Yes, I do! He is eating a carrot! Now, let me look in your mouth. Open wide, wider, wider still. Aw, come on now! Like you are yelling at your brother. There! That was a good girl." He took a culture of her throat and sent it to the lab.

It was three o'clock in the morning when the little family pulled into the driveway at home. Deborah had strep throat. The doctor said, "If Peter gets sick, just call me and I will call in a prescription for him too."

Consuelo said, "Peter, wash your face and hands really well. Brush your teeth. We will say prayers and you go right to bed."

The next morning, Consuelo called the office and gave a report of the night before about having a very sick child. She explained that she would not be coming in to work until Deborah was better. She wrapped Deborah up in a blanket, placed her in the car, and drove Peter to school.

She took Deborah back home and put her in bed. Shortly after noon, the school called and said, "Peter is sick. He is running a fever and is throwing up."

Consuelo called the doctor and told him about Peter. After picking up Peter from school, she went by the drug store, where a prescription was waiting for him. Then it was home and to care for two sick children.

She called Margaret and told her it was strep throat and now Peter had it too. Margaret said, "Johnny is throwing up and crying. I am on the way to the doctor's office with him. I understand the school has a very large number of children out sick with strep throat. So, don't feel guilty about exposing us. They caught it at school. I just hope Sarah and little Tommy don't get it. At least we know what we are dealing with."

The phone call was interrupted by Deborah, who was yelling, "I dropped my favorite toy in the toilet just as I flushed it. Water is going all over the floor. Mommy! Help!"

"Margaret, I've got to go. Sounds like Deborah has overflowed the toilet. Good grief. What next!" Deborah's screams were even louder. "Water is going everywhere!"

Frantically, Consuelo struggled to turn off the water behind the toilet. Finally, the knob was turned off. The water stopped overflowing. She attempted to use the plunger to dislodge the stuffed toy. No luck. She called Mr. Carl Hatley, the contractor, to see if he could recommend a plumber.

While she waited for the plumber to arrive, she put a pile of wet towels on the bathroom floor along with rugs to soak up water to prevent it from going down the hallway. She had used a little trash can to dip water from the toilet and dump it into the bathtub.

Soon the washer was going with hot, soapy, water working to clean more towels than a family would use in a month. She thought, something else to add to my journal. Jeff, I am glad you were not with us the past few days. You handle barf about as well as Peter. And the stuffed toy down the toilet? Like you always tell me, 'Life is never dull with kids around.'

Chapter 36

The Denali IV kept making its way slowly northward and would soon be approaching Point Barrow. During their trip, they saw a lone polar bear. Charlie and Jeff were as excited as two kids in a zoo.

The next morning, when they reached the Chukchi Sea, two crewmen rolled the two airmen out of bed at five o'clock.

They said, "The captain wants to see you topside ASAP. Do not get dressed. Get to the deck immediately!" The two crewmen escorted the two puzzled airmen to the flight deck.

They went to see what was going on. When they arrived, the captain said, "There are many traditions at sea, such as initiations, and you two flyboys are about to be initiated into the life of a seaman. This ritual excludes anyone who has been this far north and can prove it. If you guys have flown over this area, that doesn't count. Since you can't prove you have been here, you are about to be inducted into the new seamen's fraternity. Gentlemen, it is time for calisthenics."

As they began their exercises, some of the crew members came out with water hoses and hosed them down with icy cold sea water. Through chattering teeth, Jeff said, "Gentlemen, I will happily return the favor next time you are on base. I will take you for a ride of a lifetime in my airplane."

They were freezing cold. After the initiation was over, they were awarded a certificate so that, in the future, if the Denali IV should rescue them from the Russians again, they could prove they had crossed over the Arctic Circle and had reached the Chukchi Sea.

Patches of Ice were getting larger and thus creating less open water, making for slow progress. The captain said, "A major snowstorm is barreling down on the area. The temperature is already dropping. The blizzard will be hitting the area about the time we pull into port. This blizzard is early for a storm of this size. I am glad. With a little luck, we will be heading south before the dark of winter sets in. You guys may not be able to fly out for another week until this storm passes. They will probably send in a C-130 fitted with skies to pick you up. You two need to write a book about this last mission."

Josephine and Marshall were back in town, and her husband arrived home from Guam. She called the office to say that she could step back into the part-time position if Dr. Gutierrez still wanted her.

Dr. Gutierrez said, "Yes, be here tomorrow. Consuelo has sick kids and is home with them. You came back at a good time."

The office staff called and told Consuelo about Josephine's return. She was happy to have her teammate back in town, especially with her taking care of two sick kids. Plus, she thought she was getting sick too. She had fever and was aching all over.

Margaret called checking on Peter and Deborah saying Johnny was doing much better and the other two had not caught the strep.

Consuelo told her, "The kids are getting better, but I think I am catching it. I am running a fever and am aching all over. I think I will call our family doctor and talk with him about the situation. I wonder who will clean up the car if I get sick. It sure won't be Peter."

Both women laughed. Then Consuelo said, "Oh! That made my head hurt. Laughing was not a good idea. I will call you later. I need to call the doctor."

Margaret said, "If you can get an appointment today, just drop the kids off over here. Mine can't catch what they already have."

Charlie and Jeff were still chatting with the captain about what type planes fly into Point Barrow. The captain of the Denali IV responded, "I understand Regal Air flies all over the state from November to April using ski planes when necessary. When I called the port they said, 'You will be flown out of Port Barrow on one of Regal Airline's planes to Elmendorf AFB in Anchorage, Alaska, where a military plane will be waiting to fly you home.' But first this approaching blizzard has to get out of the way. As soon as we drop you guys off and take care of some business, we are heading south before we need the Russians to come rescue us!"

Consuelo called the office and said, "I am sick with strep. Yes, the children shared it with me. Josephine got back just in time. See if she can cover for me this week. This strep has really kicked my butt. I'll call when I am better. I do not think I have been this sick since college days."

Gerry called to check on her and the children. She said, "I talked with Margaret and she said your two families have had strep. Are you better?"

Consuelo said, "Yes. Thank goodness for antibiotics. We are all back going strong … well, going anyway. What about you and the colonel. What is the news around the squadron?"

"I have some news that we have known was in the works for a while. But with all that was going with several families in the squadron, we haven't said anything about it. My husband is being transferred to the Pentagon. He is to report in three months. I feel sad about leaving. I feel like I am moving away from my family."

"At times you must have felt that you had a bunch of misbehaving children mixed in the bunch. Now, you must admit that you will not miss that part! But seriously, Gerry, we all love you and will miss you. I can't stand the thought of you and the colonel not being here. I have felt that I could go to you with anything—even smokey-smelling linens." Both women laughed.

"I hope Jeff and Charlie will be home before you move on to bigger and better things."

"Yes, I am sure he will be home well before then. I know you want Jeff home as soon as possible. Thanksgiving and Christmas are looming on the horizon. It will be the best present ever to have them back home again."

Chapter 37

Pastor Johnson called to check on the family and said, "The children's department will be having a Christmas program, and they would like to know if Peter and Deborah can participate. There will be music to learn. They will be doing the Christmas story. That means they will need costumes. I am sure you can come up with a facsimile of something related to Biblical times."

Consuelo said, "The children will be delighted to participate. When does practice begin?"

"Do you think Peter will be willing to be Joseph? And Deborah is to be the star of Bethlehem. Practice will be at 7:00 p.m. tomorrow."

"I will have the children there. Thank you for calling."

Peter and Deborah were standing nearby and heard half of the conversation. They wanted to know what she was talking about with Pastor Johnson. She explained about the Christmas pageant and the parts they would play. Deborah went off into one of her pouty-foot-stomping fits.

"I don't want to be a star. I want to be a person. Why can't I be Mary? Peter gets to be something important and I don't. She crossed her arms in a defiant manner with a big frown on her face, lips pouting. "I don't want to be a star!"

Peter said, "Aw, come on, Deborah! Don't be like that. The star is important. Isn't it, Mother? Tell her."

Deborah started crying. "I wish Daddy was here. He would understand."

Consuelo said, "Come here, Deborah." With arms crossed and an ugly, frowny face, she stomped her feet and haltingly approached her mother. "Deborah, do you know what the star did? It guided the wise men across the desert and then led them straight to the Christ child. It took the wise men a long, long time to cross the desert, and the star shone over the place where angels gathered to sing, announcing the birth of Christ, and shepherds came to see the baby Jesus. Now, don't you think that is a pretty important part to play?"

By now, her arms had dropped to her sides, and she had a look of wonder on her face. She said, "Wow! The star did that? That is cool!"

"Yes, maybe tonight we can read the Christmas story, and you can both see what Joseph and the star did. Do you want to do that?"

"Mama, can you make me a super twinkly star? Maybe by then, Daddy will be home. I want him to be sure to see me. So, I want to be super twinkly just for him."

After that, the two kids disappeared down the hall, excited about their roles in the pageant. She thought, Thank you, Jesus. Another crisis headed off! Now, how do I make a super-twinkly star? Joseph, you are not a problem.

Captain Walters was listening to a radio transmission. Several miles offshore, a group of whales had become trapped in a small open area of water as a massive ice bed had begun to form. The early blizzard and a significant drop in temperature had caught the whales off guard. They could not escape from the small opening in the ice, which they used to get air. Hunters had discovered the entrapped whales. For miles, there was no open water for them to surface and breathe. Local people were attempting to keep them alive by using chainsaws to cut the ice to provide more space for the huge beasts to move about. The captain felt it was a humanitarian duty to make a channel for the big animals, so they could escape to open water. The icebreaker diverted its path to the area to lend assistance in the rescue attempt.

In the open sea, there were still patches of open water for the whales to surface. The problem was to get the big mammals to that area. The locals were bringing seals to feed the whales. There was a connection between whale and humans. The whales had scrapes on their skins from banging against the narrow icy boundaries.

When the icebreaker carefully approached the area, the whales became agitated and began floundering around, attempting to escape. The ship stayed a safe distance from the animals but had broken a path for the whales to swim to freedom. The whales seemed to sense that freedom was at hand, and, one by one, they dove under the thick ice and surfaced some distance away in the open icy waters.

Jeff and Charlie were amazed to watch the real-life drama play out. The locals waved at the whales as they disappeared from sight.

The captain said, "We need to get you guys to Point Barrow before we are marooned like those whales."

Consuelo and other mothers made costumes for the Christmas pageant. Peter's robe and staff were completed. Deborah wanted an even larger star than the one her mother had made. She wanted more glitter and twinkle lights. During practice, she wanted to be the center of attention and created a ruckus among the other children, who felt their roles were equally important. She wanted to be in every scene, whether it called for a star or not. She refused to follow instructions and was giving her leaders grief.

Pastor Johnson saw the power struggle among the small children and realized Deborah wanted to be the diva. He decided to tell the story of the birth of Christ.

"Boys and girls, will you please join me? This evening, I am going to tell you the story of Mary and Joseph, the shepherds and the angels, and the wise men. Please, come sit on the floor by me. I have a picture book that will help me tell the story. Are you comfortable? Good. Sometimes it is good to hear that very old story again to see how our play will work with it.

"This story happened a long, long time ago. At that time, King Herod was the ruler of Judea. The story is about Joseph and Mary. Mary was a virgin, and God was very pleased with her. He chose her to be the mother of Jesus. He sent one of his angels to tell her that she would give birth to Jesus. Joseph was a very good man. God chose this couple to be the earthly parents of Jesus.

"Joseph was of the lineage of the house of David. When it was time for the census to be taken, Joseph took his pregnant wife, Mary, with him when he went to Bethlehem. When they arrived in Bethlehem, Joseph tried to get a room in an inn, or a hotel, but no rooms were available. The innkeeper said they could sleep in the stable.

"During the night, baby Jesus was born. Shepherds were out in the fields taking care of their sheep when they received a surprise. The heavens were filled with angels singing and announcing the birth of Jesus. The shepherds rushed to the village to see this wondrous thing.

"Months earlier, a group of wise men in a far country had seen a bright but very quiet star that they had never seen before. They studied the star and talked with other wise men, and they concluded that the star was announcing the birth of a very important person, maybe a king of the Jews. They started their journey across the long, lonely desert. The star moved ahead of them and led them to the place where the baby king was born.

"The wise men, thinking a baby had been born to the royal family, went to see King Herod. The king didn't know what they were talking about, but he was sure he didn't want a new 'king of the Jews' living in his kingdom! He wanted to know more about this baby and where he lived. He asked them to find the baby, then come back and tell him where the child was living.

"The wise men continued on their journey, and eventually the star led them to where the young child was living, along with his parents. They gave him expensive gifts: gold, frankincense, and myrrh.

"God spoke to the wise men and said, 'Go back another way. Don't go back to see the king. He wants to harm the baby.'

"Boys and girls, where was Jesus born?"

The group said, "Bethlehem!"

"That is right. Who were the visitors who came to see the baby?" A boy answered, "Wise men and shepherds."

"Yes. What gifts did the wise men bring?" asked the pastor.

A boy said, "Gold, frankincense, and myrrh, very expensive gifts."

"What led the Wisemen to the baby Jesus?"

A girl said, "The star."

"That is right."

"What did the star do?"

"It quietly led the wise men to baby Jesus," said a girl.

"What did the star say?"

"Nothing."

"Where did the star stop?"

A child shouted, "Over the place where the baby Jesus was born."

"What did you learn from hearing this little story about the birth of Jesus?"

Peter said, "Joseph was a good man."

One of the angels said, "Angels announced the birth of Jesus Christ to the shepherds!"

One of the shepherds said, "Wow! Just think. Shepherds were the first to see the baby."

The pastor continued, "How did the star lead them to baby Jesus?"

Very softly, Deborah said, "The star led them quietly."

The icebreaker continued its journey to Point Barrow. Tension was high aboard the ship. The crew knew an intense blizzard was within less than a day away. They wanted to complete the final mission for this season and head south.

Chapter 38

Consuelo contacted her mother and Jeff's parents, asking if they could fly in when Jeff arrived home. She explained that she was making plans and wanted to know about how many might come. For now, she was checking hotels and making as many tentative arrangements as possible. Until she had a date when he would actually arrive, she could not make any concrete plans. It filled her time planning for the day when Jeff would arrive home. Until then, it was life as usual, with the kids and school plus her job.

The icebreaker continued its laborious journey to Port Barrow. The wind was picking up. Clouds were thickening. Soon the ship docked, and passengers were giving handshakes and thanks were given for the lift to land. As Jeff and Charlie disembarked, a car was there to meet them taking them to a hotel. They called their base in Guam for further instruction. Would they be debriefed in Guam or at their home base? Where would they catch a plane? As they waited the next step in their adventure, the two men worked through all the military procedures and learned how long it would be before they could be rejoined with their families.

Next, they called their families.

It was a very emotional phone call. When Consuelo answered the phone and heard Jeff's voice, she burst into tears. Peter took the phone and said, "Hello, Daddy. You were gone a long time this time. We can't wait for you to get home. I need another man in the house to balance things out. I am outnumbered! We looked up an icebreaker on the computer. And we looked up a Russian trawler too. Wow. That is a lot of exciting stuff. We can't wait for you to get home, so you can tell us all about it. I hope you have written a journal, like Mama does. Oh no, here comes Deborah! Love you, Daddy."

"Hi, Daddy. I have missed you. Guess what? I am going to be in the Christmas pageant. I am to be a star. I am a very sparkly, twinkly star. Will you be home to see the pageant? Daddy, I love you and want you to be home soon. Here is Mommy."

Consuelo had composed herself by the time she got back on the phone. They had a long and tender phone conversation. Jeff said that he would call his parents as soon as they hung up. Consuelo didn't tell him about the huge celebration she had planned and that she had invited the entire family to come when he arrived home.

Jeff said, "A huge blizzard is in progress. We are hunkered down and waiting for it to pass. Then we will fly to Anchorage. As far as I know, we will be flying back from Anchorage to Guam for debriefing and maybe meet an accident review board. We won't know about that for sure until we have been debriefed. Even then, we are not sure how long that will take. We feel certain the board has already begun their investigation. They likely will have contacted the manufacturer and obtained the video taken by a passenger aboard an airliner in the vicinity of the crash. They also have our recorded voices discussing emergency procedures and problems experienced with the plane received over communications towers and other planes in the area. But they will need to interview us. So, the wait is not over yet, but we can at least talk with each other frequently. I can't wait to get home to you and the children. Don't start making plans for a celebration party until we know how long they are going to keep us in Guam. We only hope that it will be just a few days, but one never knows."

"I am trying to hold it all together until you return." She began to cry softly. "I never gave up hope that one day you would come home to me. I just wish it was tomorrow. But we will hang on until you do walk through that door. Deborah has already announced to the world that she is, 'never, never, never, ever going to let you go away on another trip ever again!'" They both had a chuckle over that.

"How long has that blizzard been dumping bad weather on that part of the world? The children have a world globe and have a sticker on where you are. We have been trying to track you since we learned you had been on a trawler and then on an icebreaker. The children give a report almost every day at school. Oh yes, did you know that Colonel Harrison and Gerry are transferring to the Pentagon? I feel like a member of the family is moving away. They have been very supportive and helpful through so much of our assignment on this base. It is difficult to imagine not having Gerry to call in the middle of the night if one of our friends is about to deliver a baby!"

Jeff replied, "I am sure you will find someone else who will be equally helpful in such a moment."

Next, she told him about Josephine's little boy, his illness, and the imminent arrival of another baby. Four or five generations later, who would have thought this disease would show up? Doctors would be monitoring the new baby carefully watching for any signs of sickle-cell anemia.

The conversation continued until Jeff said, "I've gotta go. I still need to call my parents. I will try to call you again tomorrow."

It was a tearful goodbye. But this time, it was a goodbye with hope of being together again in the near future—whenever that might be. After the phone call ended, Consuelo went to the garage and just sat in Jeff's pickup. She prayed for him, the children, Charlie, Margaret, and the children. Last of all, she prayed that God would give her strength to carry on and not collapse under the intense pressure of trying to keep the family together.

Chapter 39

Josephine called saying, "Can you cover for me? Marshall is back in the hospital. He is in pain with a lot of swelling. His hands and feet are swollen, as are his internal organs. I am not sure how long I will be out. At least until he is stabilized again. He is not growing as he should and seems to go from infection to infection. Anyway, thanks for covering for me. I will keep you updated on our progress."

Quickly, Consuelo got ready for work, dropped the children off at school, and went to the office. When she went in, she explained why she was there and not Josephine. She was told that Josephine had called in saying that Consuelo would cover for her and explained little Marshall's struggles.

Josephine had said, "Marshall had been diagnosed with failure-to-thrive syndrome a year or so back and has been treated for that. He goes from infection to infection. My parents have closed the family home and have come down to stay with us and help with his care. Currently his little body is swollen, and he is in intense pain. He will be in for long-term care at Children's Hospital. His prognosis does not look promising. Please pray for him and for us all. We may lose him."

There was a hush and gloom over the office as each person realized the seriousness of little Marshall's condition. Everyone loved Josephine, and in such a close-knit environment, each person felt the pain of one of their own who was suffering from the possibility of losing a child.

The rest of the week, each person continued with their responsibility but held Marshal and his grave condition in the back of their minds and in their prayers. Consuelo went by Children's Hospital to visit her friend when she could and lent support and encouragement. Each day, the little fellow's condition grew worse and worse, until he could no longer fight off the disease and his frail little body quit trying to fight. He died.

It was with difficulty that the office was able to carry on duties as usual. The loss of Marshal hit everyone very hard.

The blizzard eventually drifted to another area spreading its misery as it swept the snow-covered frozen tundra. Jeff called home. He told Consuelo that a plane would be flying he and Charlie to Anchorage the following day. He would call after he reached Anchorage to let her know the next step in the process.

While the parents were talking, Peter came in and, in a very businesslike, grown-up manner, said, "Mom, can I speak to Dad? I have something very important to talk with him about. And, if I may, can I speak to him in private?"

Surprised, Consuelo responded, "Well, of course you may speak to your father. Deborah and I will be in the other room. Call me when you are finished."

"Dad, I really need to talk with you about some man issues. The boys at school say I am too old to call you Daddy, but I should call you Dad and Mom rather than Mother, Mama, or Mommy. They also talked about man things, and I wonder if what they are saying is correct. I can't wait for you to get home, so we can talk about stuff. These boys are talking about some really gross stuff, and I want to know if it is true. I can't talk with Mama … err … Mom about it because she is a girl."

"Son, I am glad you want to talk with me about these 'man things.' I want you to always come to your mother and me when you have questions. Remember, you can talk with her just the same as you can talk with me. But I understand why you want to talk with me. Talk with your mother about the things you are comfortable with, and then you and I will talk about the rest just as soon as I get home. Please promise me that you will always talk with us about any troublesome question you may have."

"I promise I will always talk with you. That is all I have for today. I look forward to seeing you soon. Love you. Mom, the phone is yours."

Deborah came bursting in and snatched the phone from his hand. "My turn. Hi, Daddy. Are you coming home? It has been so long since I have seen you. Daddy, I miss you and want you to come home."

"Love you too, little princess. I will be home just as soon as they say I can come home. You don't want me to come home any more than I want to be there. I hope to be there in time to see the Christmas pageant. Be a good girl. Love you, little princess."

"Here is Mommy."

"Here I am, and, where were we?"

"Before we go back to discussing things, let me say this. Our little guy has something very heavy on his heart. Something is troubling him. See if he will talk with you. Apparently, his buddies at school are filling him full of 'boy talk,' but I think it may be even more than that. Just consider this a little FYI about that topic. Amazing, he has turned eight years old and he is sounding so grown up.

"Now, back to us. We fly out tomorrow for Anchorage, where we will hop on a plane headed to Guam. The flight will be just under ten hours. I'll call you when I can and let you know when we arrive. We may be meeting with the accident review board. If so, it will be after we are debriefed. I will let you know when all that is completed. Then, hopefully, we will be placed on a plane bound for home."

"Do you know how long all this formality will take?"

"No, this is out of our control. We are simply pawns in the process. We will answer any questions they have to ask. By now, they will have completed the advance work of interviewing engineers from the manufacturer. They've also listened to every word we said over the airways when we were reporting our location and the problems the plane was experiencing. I am hoping they have retrieved the black box from the crash site. We will not know until we arrive before the board about how long this will take. Will it be days? Who knows? Maybe weeks. I just do not know. I can honestly say all this is making retirement look very, very good. I am feeling pretty down right now. Consuelo, I want to come home just as much as you want me there. We just have to get through this hard time. But first, you need to talk with our boy. I need to get ready to hit the road tomorrow. I wish I was there with you. I love you."

"Me too. I love you. I will talk with Peter and see what is going on in his life. He does seem very troubled. I love you too. And, yes, I like to think of the day when you can retire. Maybe we can go help your brother at the family mechanic shop. This has been a rough better part of a year. Hopefully, you will be home in time for the Christmas program. The kids are so cute, playing their parts. I love you. Rest well tonight. Call me when you can. Love you. Bye."

After the children had their baths, stories were read, and prayers said. Consuelo tucked Deborah in bed and then went into Peter's room. She said, "Little buddy, what is wrong? You seem to be carrying the weight of the world on your shoulders. How can I help you—or can I help you?"

His lower lip started to quiver. "It is about Joey and his little sister, Mary Lou."

"What about your friends? Are they all right?"

By now, tears were trickling down his cheeks. "No, they are not all right. Their daddy has been in Afghanistan for six months. Their mother has a boyfriend who has moved into their house until their daddy comes back. He is doing bad things to Mary Lou and makes Joey watch. Their mother is drunk and doesn't know what is happening. Even when Mary Lou screams for help, their mother doesn't help her. When Joey tries to fight the man, he gets knocked down. Joey showed us his bruises. Mommy, what can I do?"

"Little buddy, you have done exactly what you are supposed to do. You told me! I know what to do. I will make some phone calls. Joey and Mary Lou will get the help they need. Thank you for telling me. Always tell your daddy or me when you have a problem. We are your parents, and parents are supposed to be there for their kids. I love you, little buddy. Oh, one thing more, you said, 'He showed us his bruises.' Which other boys did he show?"

"Billy, Sammy, Pedro, and Jose. One more thing. The boys at school say that I am too big to say Mother or Mommy or Mama or Daddy. They say I should say Dad and Mom. Is it okay if I say Dad or Mom? Or should I say Mama, Mommy, or Mother and Daddy?"

"You call us what you are most comfortable with. We know you love us, and you know we love you. So, Dad and Mom are fine with us. Love you, little buddy."

Consuelo called the principal of the school as well as the school counselor to inform them of the problem she had just learned about. "The other boys who saw Joey's bruises are Bill, Sammy, Pedro, and Jose," she reported. "Sammy lives across the street from Joey."

From there, the system was put into motion to give two helpless children the help they desperately needed.

The next day, when Peter went to school, Billy, Sammy, Pedro, and Jose were there to meet him, but not Joey. The boys were in a huddle when Peter walked up.

Sammy was talking. "Two police cars and another car went to Joey's house last night. The police took that man away. He was in his underwear. Joey's mother came out the door cussing the police for not minding their own business. She couldn't even walk straight. Then the police arrested her too. She was yelling, cussing, kicking, and fighting them. Joey and Mary Lou were taken with a lady in another car. Joey and Mary Lou were holding on to each other and looked scared."

The friends stood quietly thinking about what their friends had told them.

Sammy said, "My dad said, 'Maybe their dad will be brought back early because of this family problem.'"

The four friends stood in silence thinking about their friend and wondering if they would ever see him again.

Chapter 40

Consuelo was at the office in the snack room visiting with other staff members before patients started arriving. She said, "Too much heavy stuff has happened the past few months. I am not sure how much more I can stand. I hate to complain, but I am stressed. Josephine lost her little boy, last night friends of my kids were removed from the home by CPS because of family problems, and now my husband is being sent back to Guam to complete business related to the crash before he is released to come home. Sorry to say this, but I am emotionally drained!"

Several staff members, including Doctors Swarovski and Hielaman, came over to give her a hug. Dr. Gutierrez said, "I would have lost it a long time ago. I admire you for the way you are holding up, but you must suck it up and hold on a little longer. This too shall pass. Jeff will soon be home. Surely, they will not keep him there any longer than is necessary. You have two little guys who are looking to you to maintain the status quo. You don't have a choice. You have to do this. You are made of good stuff, Consuelo. You can do it."

One of the nurses came over and said, "Here is some chocolate. I prescribe you eat this whole candy bar! I guarantee it will make you feel better." Everyone laughed.

Consuelo said, "I like your brand of medicine."

The day was a busy one. Soon it was time to pick up the children at school. When she drove to the usual place in front of the school, the children were there waiting for her.

Peter was first in the car. He said, "Mom, guess what? Sammy said that last night, two police cars and one other car were at Joey's house. That man was arrested. His mother was cussing and kicking and fighting the police. Sammy said all the neighbors were outside their houses watching. He said Joey and Mary Lou looked scared. Mommy ... err, Mom, did they get help?"

"Yes, Peter. They will be taken care of. There are trained people to help them. They are safe now."

Deborah said, "What happened? Is Mary Lou all right? I really like her. I didn't see her at school today."

In a mature tone of voice, Peter said, "Yes, she and Joey are alright now."

Deborah responded, "Okay. I am glad. Did you know that my teacher's dog had puppies? She had four boy puppies and three girl puppies. Can we have a puppy?"

Consuelo was relieved that Deborah had steered the conversation to a much more relaxed subject.

When they arrived home, the children were playing with neighborhood kids. Consuelo called Josephine. It had been several days since she had checked on her. She learned her pregnancy was progressing right on target. Josephine was still struggling with the gigantic loss of a child. Consuelo asked if she had contacted a support group of people who were recovering from the loss of a child. Josephine said, "I am not to a point where I can do that yet. In time, perhaps, I can do that—in the future."

The two women visited for several minutes before the conversation drew to a close. Next, she called Gerry. "How are transfer plans progressing?"

Gerry replied, "I am attempting to de-clutter and give away things we have not used in a while. Would you believe I've found boxes that haven't been unpacked since we moved here? Do you think I need those things?"

Consuelo responded, "Before you give those boxes to Goodwill, you might want to check. There might be something of value—heirlooms, gold, silver, or something."

Both women laughed.

Consuelo said, "Tell the colonel that Jeff is flying back to Guam for debriefing and perhaps a meeting with the accident review board. I am sure he knows already, but just in case. Anyway, I hope this investigation will not be prolonged. Oh yes, I talked with Josephine. She is still struggling in her grief. She said her pregnancy is advancing well."

The two friends talked for a few minutes as Consuelo prepared the evening meal. She concluded, "I need to call the children in for dinner. I have enjoyed chatting. Say 'hi' to the colonel."

CHAPTER 41

Jeff and Charlie arrived in Guam. They were told the agenda and time to report the next day. Both were exhausted, and they fell into bed and into a deep sleep. The last thought in their minds was *Soon this nightmare will be over.*

The debriefing was scheduled for 0900. The findings of the debriefing would determine whether an accident review board would be convened.

Jeff called. "I can't talk very long. I just wanted you to know that the guys had recorded the international musical program that was in progress when our plane went down. Charlie and I watched the program today while we waited for our debriefing. I must say, this Navajo was green with envy when I watched my beautiful wife dancing with Major Jose Ramirez."

She laughed. "I am glad they saved the video for you."

When Peter and Deborah came in to breakfast, Deborah asked, "Did Daddy call last night?" Consuelo replied, "No, but he did call for a couple of minutes this morning. Hopefully, he will call again today. Maybe he will have some idea of when he is coming home. We can hope anyway. Go brush your teeth and grab your things. Time to go to school."

All day, Consuelo kept watching the clock, wondering what was happening for Jeff and Charlie. She kept praying, *Lord, please help things to go smoothly for Jeff and Charlie. Please bring them home to us.*

When she picked up the children after school, she said, "Let's call Margaret and see if she and the children would like to go out to eat with us tonight."

Deborah said, "Oh no! Last time we did that I got sick."

"Deborah, don't remind me of that!" Peter shouted.

Consuelo laughed. "Okay, okay. So, I had a bad idea. We will go home and have fish sticks for dinner. Does anybody have homework?"

Peter moaned. "Yes. I have math problems to do."

Deborah whispered, "I am to read five pages of my book, but I need somebody to help me."

"Okay, you two can go play for twenty minutes, then do homework while I cook supper."

Consuelo grabbed an armful of laundry to throw in the washer. She tidied up the house and was getting ready to go to the kitchen when her phone rang. It was Jeff. Excitedly she said, "Jeff, it is you! Tell me, how did your day go? What do you know?"

"Hi yourself. I had a good day. The debriefing went really well. They had done a lot of advance work and studies. They recovered the black box and saw that we did all the emergency procedures according to the manual. They were pleased. Consequently, there will be no accident review board. I am coming home!"

"When are you to arrive home? I have been talking with the family, and everyone is coming in to welcome you. I have contacted hotels and have received a group rate. When they heard it was for your family, they gave me a military discount in addition to the group rate. They will come in for a couple of days. We plan to give you a welcome like you have never had before. Oh, Jeff, I can't wait to see you. When will you arrive?"

"The day after tomorrow. Maybe the family can come in for the weekend. If they can't get flights that soon, then maybe next week."

"That's fine. Are you calling them when we get off the phone? If you do, tell them that I will be calling them later. Jeff, I can't wait to see you. My head is spinning. I want to have the biggest welcome home party this neighborhood has ever seen. I can see it now. I will be making notes, planning food and lists of people to invite all night tonight. I am so excited!"

Jeff laughed loudly. "Just being home with you and the kids will be enough welcome home party for me!" "Call me as soon as you know when you are leaving Guam and when you will arrive home. I don't care if it is in the middle of the night."

"Did I tell you that I will be flying home nonstop in a commercial plane? This time, I am not riding home in a C-130, like the last time I flew back from Guam. I would have been very happy to be flying with those guys if it meant I would be flying home. Listen to us! We sound like two giddy teenagers!"

"Will you have some leave time? Let me know so I can take off from work at the same time."

Peter came through the door. "I'm starving. When is dinner going to be ready? Hey! Are you talking with daddy?" Jumping up and down, he added, "My turn!"

Laughing, Consuelo said, "My phone has been hijacked by a short person. Love you."

"Hi, Daddy. I mean Dad! When are you coming home? Oh great! That gives me time to clean my room. I can't wait to see you. I have to tell you that I told Mom about what was bothering me. She made some phone calls. Things are better for Joey and Mary Lou, and that man was arrested, and their mom was arrested too. Joey and Mary Lou went with someone Mom called CPS. I think the CPS was calling their Daddy's mother to come get them. I'll tell you all about it when you get home. I better go get started on my room. It will take me until the time you get home to have it picked up. Can't wait to see you."

Deborah came storming through the door. "Where is Peter? Are you eating without me? What are you doing?" With big eyes and an excited look on her face, she asked, "Are you talking to Daddy? Nobody told me that he had called. Give me the phone. It's my turn. Hi, Daddy. When are you coming home? Oh yeah! When you come home, and you and Mommy are dancing, if we stay up late, I promise I will not be grumpy the next day. Oh, Daddy. I want to see you right now! I can't wait! I never, never, never, never want you to go away again. We were so scared. On TV, we saw your plane blow up. I prayed to God, 'Please don't let my daddy be dead,' and God heard my prayer. Daddy, I love you. I have to go tell all my friends. My daddy is coming home!"